"Do you realize you could've been killed?" Matt asked.

"I—I'm doing my job. I was following a lead for a story. I just wanted to see what I could find out," Rachel said.

Matt's heart beat faster with each word she spoke. He raked his hand through his hair and stared at her. "You should've called me right away and told me about this. I warned you about the danger. Whoever shot these guys was shooting at you, too."

Even in the dim light he could see the fear that flashed in her eyes before she squared her shoulders and took a deep breath. "He was firing at you, too," she said.

"His aim would've been better if he'd intended to hit me."

Rachel nodded. "He probably could have hit me, too, if he'd really wanted to kill me. Why do you think he did that?"

Matt shrugged. "Probably just wanted to scare us."

Well, the shooter had accomplished *that* much.

Books by Sandra Robbins

Love Inspired Suspense

Final Warning
Mountain Peril
Yuletide Defender

SANDRA ROBBINS,

a former teacher and principal in the Tennessee public schools, is a full-time writer for the Christian market. She is married to her college sweetheart, and they have four children and five grandchildren. As a child, Sandra accepted Jesus as her Savior and has depended on Him to guide her throughout her life.

While working as a principal, Sandra came in contact with many individuals who were so burdened with problems that they found it difficult to function in their everyday lives. Her writing ministry grew out of the need for hope that she saw in the lives of those around her.

It is her prayer that God will use her words to plant seeds of hope in the lives of her readers. Her greatest desire is that many will come to know the peace she draws from her life verse, Isaiah 40:31—."But those who hope in the Lord will renew their strength. They will soar on wings like eagles, they will run and not grow weary, they will walk and not be faint."

And they that know thy name will put their trust in thee: for thou, Lord, hast not forsaken them that seek thee.

—*Psalms* 9:10

To Kristi, Marti, Stacey and Scott

The joy you bring me makes every day
seem like Christmas.

YULETIDE DEFENDER

SANDRA ROBBINS

Steeple
Hill®

Published by Steeple Hill Books™

STEEPLE HILL BOOKS

Steeple Hill®

Recycling programs for this product may not exist in your area.

ISBN-13: 978-0-373-44423-6

YULETIDE DEFENDER

Copyright © 2010 by Sandra Robbins

www.SteepleHill.com

Printed in U.S.A.

ONE

Arriving at a murder scene before breakfast wasn't Rachel Long's idea of a good way to start the day.

She leaned against the lamppost at the corner of Ninth and Perkins and pulled her coat tighter. The December wind that whistled around the deserted storefronts and run-down apartment buildings lining the street sent a shiver down her spine. Unlike other neighborhoods in Lake City, there were no holiday decorations anywhere in sight. In fact, nothing about her surroundings gave a hint that Christmas was only a few weeks away.

A young man's lifeless body sprawled twenty feet away spoke volumes about what life was like in this part of the city. Several uniformed policemen stood to the side as crime scene investigators gathered their evidence.

Her stomach rumbled and she pressed her hand against her abdomen to suppress the hunger pains. Coffee would have to come later. As chief investigative reporter for the *Lake City Daily Beacon,* her job was to cover the news.

One of the policemen backed away, and Rachel caught sight of the victim's leg twisted underneath him. She made a quick note in her journal of his white canvas tennis shoe with a five-pointed star on the side—one of the identifying marks of the Vipers, the gang that boasted control of this neighborhood.

She pursed her lips and tried to mentally recall how many

gang-related deaths she'd reported in the past two months. Four? No, five. This one made the sixth victim.

A car pulled to a stop across the street and Detective Matt Franklin stepped out from the driver's side. He tugged at the cuffs of a white shirt and they slipped over his wrists from underneath the sleeves of his navy blazer. Even this early in the morning he looked like he belonged in a fashion magazine spread. The wind ruffled his brown hair. He smoothed it into place as he waited for the man who climbed from the passenger side of the car.

"Matt," Rachel called out.

He stopped in the middle of the street and glanced around. Catching sight of her, he turned and walked toward her. The corners of his eyes crinkled with a smile. He stopped in front of her and tilted his head to one side. "Rachel, how did you find out about this so quickly?"

"My scanner." She glanced toward the group examining the body. "Another gang killing?"

He sighed and nodded. "Looks like it."

"I noticed the boy's tennis shoes. He's a member of the Vipers. Do you think this is the work of the Rangers?"

Matt shrugged. "It's too early to know. Some in the department think the Vipers from the north side of the city and the Rangers from the south have decided to declare open war on each other. But so far neither gang is talking."

"May I quote you on that?"

"You probably would even if I said no." His mouth curved into the lopsided smile she'd first noticed when they met two months ago at the scene of the first gang member's death.

Rachel closed the notebook she held and dropped her pen into her bag. "When I was growing up, I never thought we'd someday have two gangs in a town this size. They were in urban areas like New York and Los Angeles, not in a small city in the heart of Illinois."

Matt nodded. "No town, no matter how small, is safe from

the threat of gangs. Pressure from large-city police departments is forcing many gang members from the cities into more rural areas. Once there, they recruit locals into the groups. It's a growing problem all across the country."

Rachel glanced back at the body down the street. "So now we have six kids dead. Three Rangers and three Vipers. And because of what? Their neighborhoods aren't any better because they died. In fact, now it's worse for the people who live there and want to raise their children in a safe environment." She shook her head. "What a waste."

Matt regarded her with a steady gaze. "I didn't realize you had such strong feelings about the fate of these kids."

Her eyes grew wide. "Of course I do. Most of them don't have a chance of escaping their lives of poverty. They're looking to neighborhood gangs to save them and instead they're ending up dead."

Matt's gaze flitted across her face for a moment before he responded. "Once they take that step into the gang life, though, they're also dangerous. When I saw you standing over here, I thought it might be a good time to give you a friendly warning. You've written some hard-hitting articles in the past few weeks since this string of killings started. I'd hate to see you anger the wrong people."

She shrugged. "I don't make the news. I only report it."

Matt nodded. "I know. And I don't make the crimes. I only try to solve them. All I'm saying is just don't get in over your head."

Rachel smiled. "It's nice of you to worry about my safety, but I don't think I'll have any problems. The gang members only know me as a name in the newspaper. I doubt if they even care what I think."

Matt shook his head. "I don't know about that. Your picture is right beside your byline. Someone wanting to find you wouldn't have to look far."

Rachel had never thought of that, and her skin tingled with

a rush of fear. "Don't try to scare me, Matt. I can't back off my job. Good reporters follow the facts and print them."

Matt's dark eyes clouded. "I know what these gangs are like, Rachel. I deal with them on a daily basis. As a friend, I thought I should warn you. Just be careful."

She nodded. "I will be. And don't forget to read my story." She glanced around at the local residents, some in their pajamas and robes, standing along the sidewalk. "I think I'll try to get some quotes from a few of the people who live around here. Of course they'll refuse to give their names, but you can't blame them. They're afraid of retaliation from the people who control their streets."

"We run into that problem all the time. It sure makes catching a killer harder." Matt glanced over his shoulder at the crime scene. "Well, I'd better get busy. I just wanted to pass along my concern." He turned to leave but then he faced her again. "By the way, I saw you at church last Sunday with your friend Mindy. You left before I could speak to you."

Rachel smiled at how surprised she'd been to see Matt there. That day he was dressed in jeans and a knit shirt as he played the drums in the praise band for the worship service. He'd looked so relaxed and completely absorbed in the music. Today he was every inch the professional policeman.

"Mindy has been after me to go with her, so I did."

"Maybe you'd like to come to our Singles Bible Study. We meet tonight."

She shrugged. "Maybe. If I have time. My job keeps me busy."

He looked back at the crime scene. "Mine does, too. I'd better get to work. See you later."

Rachel watched as Matt jogged back to the officers still beside the body. She'd liked Matt the first time they'd met. Perhaps it was the sorrow she saw in his eyes as he gazed down at the young victim who'd died alone on a dark street. And now a sixth person had also met his end.

She turned her attention to the small crowd of onlookers who'd gathered in front of an apartment building across the street. At the edge of the cluster of residents, a woman who appeared to be in her early thirties gripped the hand of a young boy beside her.

As Rachel watched, the woman spoke to the boy who stared into her face. The child didn't move as the woman accented her words with gestures toward the body across the street.

Fascinated by the exchange between the two, Rachel ambled toward them until she stood in front of the woman. She smiled. "Good morning, my name is Rachel Long. I'm a reporter for the *Lake City Daily Beacon*, and I noticed you standing here. I wondered if I might speak with you."

Suspicion flashed in the woman's eyes and she gripped the boy's hand tighter. "What about?"

Rachel glanced at the boy. "Is this your son?"

The woman straightened her shoulders. "Yes."

"I couldn't help but notice that you were talking to him as if you really wanted to impress something on him. It reminded me of how my mother used to talk with me."

The woman pointed across the street. "I was tellin' him that he's all I got in this world, and I don't aim to see him end up dead on no street corner. That's what gangs do for you. Promise all kinds of things but they ain't true."

Rachel nodded. "You're a very wise woman. I know it isn't easy living in a neighborhood where gangs roam the streets."

The woman's eyes grew wide and her mouth pulled into a grim line. "Easy? There ain't nothing easy 'bout life around here, and these hoodlums with their drugs and guns just make it harder for folks like us who workin' to get by."

"Do you have something you'd like to say to the people of Lake City or to the police about what the gangs are doing to our city?"

She started to speak but stopped. Fear flashed in her

eyes. "You ain't gonna use my name or tell where I live, are you?"

Rachel shook her head. "I'll just quote you as a concerned mother."

"Well, then I guess I'd say to the folks who live in the nice neighborhoods, you ain't got no idea what it's like to be afraid of where you live. My son can't play outside 'cause I'm scared a stray bullet gonna hit him. We don't get out after dark, just stay inside with all the curtains pulled. And we stay away from the windows. I can't afford to move nowhere else, so I'm stuck here. When is somebody gonna help us clean up the filth that's turned what used to be a good neighborhood into a battlefield?"

Rachel had promised herself when she became a reporter that she would keep her personal feelings under control when she was interviewing someone. The anguish in this mother's eyes, though, made her forget that intention.

Her heart pricked at the predicament of this woman and her child. She blinked back the moisture in her eyes and smiled down at the boy. "You have a smart mama. Do what she says and stay safe."

The boy's somber brown eyes stared at her. "I will."

The mother pulled her son closer. "You gonna write how bad it is down here?"

"I am." She reached out and squeezed the woman's hand that rested on her son's shoulder. "I'll be thinking of you."

With a sigh she headed back across the street. She saw Matt bending over the victim. He straightened and smiled when he saw her. They stared at each other for a moment before they both waved, and Rachel turned down the street to the spot where she'd parked.

When she climbed into her car and cranked the engine, she held her breath. To her relief, the motor purred to life. She really had to do something about a car soon. Hers had already exceeded its life expectancy by a few years. Maybe by this time next year she'd be driving a new vehicle.

The *Beacon* was just the first step to success. If things went as planned, this job would be her springboard to a larger newspaper or even a television station. And stories of rival gangs killing each other just might be the ticket to jump-start the journey.

Rachel thought again of the mother's fear for her son. Her own mother had dealt with many problems in raising Rachel and her sister, but gangs weren't something they had to worry about. She couldn't imagine what life must be like for that woman and her son. Maybe if she dug deeper into the killings, she would find something to help the police.

Matt's warning drifted through her mind but she shook it away. There were reasons why she wanted to succeed at her job. No, *had* to succeed. She only had one choice—to go anywhere and talk to anybody to get the story she needed.

Rachel stared at the computer screen and scanned the article she'd just written once more before sending it to the copy editor. "It seems almost like a rewrite of the other murders," she grumbled aloud.

She leaned back in her chair and tapped the desktop with a pencil. The police might believe gang violence was the reason for the similar killings, but according to what Matt had told her they still couldn't be sure. With no clues left behind, the police didn't appear to know where to turn. Gang members weren't talking, and most residents who lived in the neighborhoods controlled by the groups were too afraid to tell what they knew.

Somebody in Lake City knew what was going on with these killings but so far no one had come forward. She reread the last two lines of the article she'd just completed. "It's time for every resident of Lake City to say, 'We will not stand quietly by and let the gangs destroy us.' Only by joining forces can we safeguard the future and provide a secure way of life for our children and those who will come after us."

Whether or not her call for unity would work, she didn't know. All she could do was try to rally the citizens to fight what was happening around them. She sighed and, with a click of the mouse, sent the story on its way to the copy editor.

She picked up her coffee cup and took a drink just as the phone rang. Setting the cup back on the desk, she wedged the receiver between her ear and shoulder. "Rachel Long. May I help you?"

"I don't know. Maybe I can help you." Rachel's eyes widened at the curtness in the man's voice. This was no friendly call. She pushed her cup away, reached for a pencil and slid her notepad across her desk.

"Help me with what?"

"I been reading your stories in the paper."

Rachel took a deep breath to still her thudding heart. "Which ones?"

"The gang murders."

Rachel's fingers flexed and gripped the pencil tighter. "I'm glad. We always like to hear from our readers."

"I ain't calling to brag on your writing. I gots a story I want to talk about."

She poised the pencil above the pad. "And what's your name?"

A low laugh came over the phone. "That don't matter. Let's just say I'm a confidential source. Okay?"

Rachel could almost hear her heart pounding. "That depends on what you have to tell me."

"Oh, you gonna like this. 'Cause I got a story that'll rock this city."

"I'll have to be the judge of that. Now tell me what you've got."

"No way. You ain't gittin' this information over the phone. You gonna have to meet me in person."

The sinister tone of the man's voice sent chills down her spine. Matt's warning flashed into her mind. Could this be a gang member? If so, she could be walking straight into trouble if she agreed to meet him.

On the other hand, if she didn't meet him, she might be giving up the chance at the break she'd been waiting for. A huge story could get her name out there to influential people in the industry. When she weighed the pros and cons of the situation, she knew it was a no-brainer. She hesitated only a moment before she answered.

"Okay, where do you want me to meet you?"

"You know the City Park out on Highway 45?"

"Yes."

"Meet me there at midnight. Go to the picnic tables by the lake and sit on the bench right next to the woods. And come alone. Understand?"

Rachel swallowed. "Yes."

The caller disconnected with a click. Rachel replaced the phone and stared into space. Somehow she'd known since the first murder that this was the story she'd been waiting for—one that would set her apart as an investigative reporter. And one that would prove she was unafraid to pursue truth, no matter where it took her.

Dangerous or not, she had to go. This could be just what she'd been waiting for—her big break. Or it might be more— the tragic end of a promising career.

The bells in the pavilion tower across the lake chimed the midnight hour as Rachel climbed from the car. The familiar landscape looked very different than it did in the daytime, when families played together in the wide expanse. Rachel shivered at the stillness that enveloped her.

The distant rumble of thunder broke the silence. She glanced up at dark clouds rolling across the sky. The moon disappeared behind a cloud and the darkness deepened. The streetlamps around the lake cast a soft glow of light on the jogging trail that circled it. Tonight, however, there were no runners. She was alone.

She studied the park benches that dotted the grassy area in back of the picnic tables, then trudged toward them and scanned the dark forest beyond for signs of movement. Seeing nothing, she eased onto the bench where he'd instructed her to sit.

The leaves on the trees behind her rustled and she tensed. Was there someone there? She tilted her head to the side and listened. An owl hooted and she shivered.

How long should she give him to show up? She hugged her coat tighter and knew she'd stay until sunrise if she had to.

"Don't turn around."

She gasped in surprise as fingers clamped down on her shoulder. Fear oozed through her body and left a blanket of ice in its wake. "W-who a-are y-you?"

"Don't make no difference what my name is." His warm breath fanned the back of her neck.

Rachel struggled to breathe. "Then what shall I call you?"

"Like I said, just say I'm your confidential source." He paused for a moment before he continued, "I been readin' your stories 'bout gang members being killed. You done a good job reportin' the facts."

"Do you have some additional information for me?"

"Maybe." His fingers tightened on her shoulder. "Let's see now, in that last story, how many you say died?"

When Rachel didn't answer, his index finger jabbed her. She gulped a big breath of air and sat up straighter. "Five before today. Now there's six. All of them shot to death. The police think rival gangs are killing each other."

The man behind her exhaled a long breath. "The popo don't know nothing."

Rachel frowned and tilted her head. "You mean the police?"

"Yeah."

"What makes you think that"

"It ain't what I *think*. It's what I *know*." His lips grazed her ear.

His nicotine-scented breath filled her nostrils and she turned her head away. "And what's that?" Rachel asked.

"They's two gangs here in Lake City, the Vipers and the Rangers. The Vipers, them are my brothers. We take care of our hood. The Rangers, they on the south side of town, and we don't mess with them."

Rachel started to say she knew how the Vipers took care of their neighborhood—drugs, shootings, robberies—but reason told her not to anger him. "I know about the two."

"If they found out I was talkin' to you, I'd be dusted by mornin'." A trace of fear trembled through the man's words.

"Your friends would kill you? Why?"

A small groan came from behind her. "We ain't 'posed to talk to nobody 'bout gang business."

"Oh."

"The popo think the gangs be fightin' each other in a war. That ain't true, but I 'spect somebody wants to start one." He paused for a moment and Rachel tensed, wondering if he expected her to say something. When she remained silent, he continued, "You 'member the last murder two weeks ago? The Viper that was killed in front of that pizza place on First Street?"

"Yes, I wrote a story about it."

"Well, what you didn't write was that there was another guy with the one killed, but the shooter missed him."

Rachel thought back to the story. No mention had been made by the police about another individual being present. "Who was it?"

"Me. I saw the guy right before he shot and he weren't no

gang member. I ran and he chased me. I hid in a Dumpster, but I seen him."

"Then you can identify the killer?"

"Naw, but I knows he's a white guy."

Rachel's shoulders sagged. "That just reinforces what the police think. The Rangers are white. It was one of their members."

"No," he hissed. "This guy didn't have no flag."

Rachel sat up straighter and frowned. "He wasn't wearing gang colors?"

"No. If he been a Ranger, he would've been proud of the hit and woulda been showing 'em off."

Rachel thought about that for a moment. What he said made sense. "Then who do you think he was?"

"Ain't got no idea. But like I said, I been thinkin'. The popo ain't questioned why they so many deaths of gang members in Lake City all of a sudden. They say that just no-goods killin' each other. What if somebody who ain't in a gang'd like to see the two go head-to-head in a war? So he starts killin' Vipers and Rangers, hoping that'll happen."

Rachel's eyes widened. "A vigilante? You think there's one on the loose in Lake City?"

"Now you catchin' on."

"But why are you telling me this? Why not go to the police?"

A laugh rumbled in the man's throat. "I can't do that 'cause we don't talk to no popo. They wish we'd all disappear from the face of the earth anyway. I expect they figures if we kill each other off it'll just make their job easier."

Rachel's breath caught in her throat. A vigilante? She'd never thought of that. "What do you want me to do?"

He leaned closer, and she could feel him pressing against the back of the bench. "I'm tired of the killin'. I wants you to write a story 'bout what I told you. Then see what happens."

Rachel shook her head. "I can't do that just because it's what you believe. I need some kind of evidence."

Out of the corner of her eye, she saw an arm appear next to her shoulder. A piece of paper dangled from long brown fingers before it fluttered to the bench beside her. "This here the name of a cop on the take and where he meets up with a Ranger for his payoff. He'll be there at midnight tomorrow night. Check this out first. See if I'm tellin' the truth about this. Then maybe you'll believe me about the vigilante."

Rachel reached for the paper. "Okay. How do I get in touch with you if this lead proves true?"

The man laughed. "Don't worry. I be watchin', and I gonna be callin' you 'cause there's somethin' I want out of this."

Goose bumps raced up Rachel's arm. "And what's that?"

"I wants you to help me get outta town. Start a new life somewheres else." He was silent for a moment. "I know the gang life ain't for me no more. I wish things would change, but I done decided ain't nothin' gonna change where I live 'til Jesus comes back."

A gasp escaped Rachel's throat. "Are you a believer?"

He exhaled a long breath. "My mama taught me lots of stuff. Don't think she's too proud of me now, though."

His words felt like a kick in the stomach. She knew what it was like to disappoint your mother. "If you're really serious, I'll help you whether or not the story pans out."

"I knowed you was a good woman. I be talkin' to you."

"Wait! Don't go!" she said. However she sensed no one stood behind her any longer. She counted to ten before she slowly turned and stared at the tree line behind the bench. Again she was alone in a deserted park.

She grabbed the piece of paper, stuck it in her pocket and ran toward her car. Once inside she locked the door and leaned her head against the steering wheel. Tonight she'd been more scared than at any other time since she had begun working at the newspaper.

She straightened in the seat, pulled the paper from her pocket and stared at it. *Walters and Branson.* Another street corner on the run-down south side of town.

Her hand shook and she jammed the paper back into her pocket. She had no idea what would happen tomorrow night, but she did know one thing. She'd be there to witness whatever took place.

TWO

Matt Franklin glanced at his watch as he walked down the hallway at the Lake City Youth Center. 1:00 a.m.? Where had the time gone? When he'd dropped by after the Bible study, he'd only meant to stay a few minutes, but he'd soon lost himself in planning next week's activities for the young boys he mentored. A light in the staff break room caught his attention and he stopped at the door.

David Foreman, the center's director, sat at the round table in the middle of the room. He sipped from a cup of coffee but looked up and motioned for Matt to enter. "What are you doing here so late? You had a busy day with this latest murder. You must be dead on your feet."

Matt walked to the table and pulled out the chair across from David. "I didn't mean to stay so long. I thought you'd already left. I heard you go out the back door several hours ago."

David nodded toward the counter where the coffeepot sat. "I wanted some coffee and there wasn't any left in the canister. I went down the street to that all-night market and got some. I knew the staff wouldn't like it if they didn't get their fix tomorrow morning."

Matt couldn't suppress the yawn that overwhelmed him. He tried to cover his mouth. "Sorry about that. I guess I'm more tired than I thought. But I'm used to missing sleep. It seems to go with my job."

"You need to take care of yourself, Matt." David regarded him for a moment. "Don't you have a life outside of the police department and the Center? I appreciate your help, but you spend most of your off-duty hours here. Isn't there some nice woman that you could take out every once in a while?"

Matt chuckled. "I haven't found one yet. Maybe I will." He swallowed before he dared voice what he'd wanted to ask David for several days. "I have met an interesting woman, though. Rachel Long. I think you know her."

David's eyebrows arched. "Rachel? She's my goddaughter. I've been a friend of her mother's since we were children. In fact, I helped Rachel get her job at the *Beacon*. So you're interested in Rachel?"

Matt straightened in his chair and clasped his hands on top of the table. "I don't know. She just seems nice. I thought she might come to the Bible study tonight, but she didn't show up."

David shook his head. "Sounds like her. She hasn't gone to church much since she got out from under her mother's influence. I guess it's a kind of rebellion for being made to go all the time when she was younger." David paused and ran his index finger around the rim of the coffee cup. "All she thinks about is work and how she wants to make a name for herself at the paper."

"I've noticed she's really dedicated to her job."

David chuckled. "Dedicated is hardly the word for it. Obsessed describes it better."

Although Matt had talked to Rachel several times, he'd never suspected she might be so driven to succeed. "But why?"

"It has to do with her family."

Matt nodded. "Oh, I see."

If there was anything he understood, it was how a family

could influence the way a person approached life. He should know. His life was the perfect example of what a dysfunctional family could do to a person. Thankfully, he'd escaped them and found God in the process.

Matt pushed back from the table and stood. "Maybe she'll get active in the church."

David picked up the cup and took a sip. As he put it down, he smiled at Matt. "Or make new friends there that will occupy some of her time."

Matt's face burned, and he stuck his hands in his pockets. "Maybe so. Well, I guess I'd better get on home. I'll see you later."

As he walked to the parking lot, Matt thought about what David had said. Maybe Rachel was so involved with her job that she didn't want anything else.

After they first met, he knew he wanted to know her better. He'd been in the middle of giving the local television station a statement about one of the gang-related murders when she had walked up beside the cameraman and proceeded to write down every word he said.

The sun had sparkled on her shoulder-length blond hair, and she had chewed on her lips in concentration, nodding every once in a while as if she agreed with what he was saying. When she had glanced up, her piercing blue eyes had stared at him with an intensity that made his heart do flip-flops. Then she had smiled, and he couldn't finish his interview quickly enough. He had to find out more about this willowy blonde who took his breath away.

Now two months later, he still knew very little about her. One of the reasons for going over to her at the crime scene today had been to ask her to go with him to the ballet at the Fox Theater. Instead he'd lost his nerve and they'd discussed the murder.

He reached his car and climbed inside. Weariness surged through his body. He hoped he wouldn't be called out tonight for the murder of another kid. This last one had been younger than the others, not much over sixteen. It troubled him to think of the wasted lives he'd seen in the past few weeks. Gang violence in Lake City was escalating out of control and he had to help the department find a way of stopping it.

There had to be a solution, but what it was he didn't know yet.

The next morning, Rachel strode down the hallway of the Lake City Police Department toward the open office door a uniformed officer had pointed out. She peered inside at Matt Franklin. He looked tired this morning. His dark eyes, usually filled with excitement, appeared bloodshot.

The pencil he held dropped to the pile of papers in front of him. He yawned, rubbed his hands across his eyes and then ran his fingers through his thick dark hair. She knocked on the door frame. "Good morning. Are you up to having a visitor?"

His eyes lit up when he saw her. "Rachel? What are you doing here?" He rose and came around his desk.

She laughed, dropped her briefcase on the floor and shrugged out of her coat. "You look tired this morning. Did you work last night?"

He shook his head. "No, I went to the Bible study at church, then dropped by the Youth Center to do some work." He took her coat, hung it on the rack and pulled out a chair for her. Walking behind his desk, he sat down and folded his hands on the top. "And to what do I owe the pleasure of a visit from Lake City's favorite investigative reporter so early in the morning?"

Rachel chuckled. "Favorite reporter? I don't know about that. You should see some of the emails I get. You might change your mind."

Matt's tired eyes twinkled. "If they're anything like mine, I completely understand. If we don't solve a crime, we're wasting the taxpayers' money. If we do make an arrest, the jailed person's friends think we're persecuting him. Sometimes it's a no-win situation."

Rachel nodded. "I guess we have something in common."

Matt smiled. "So tell me, what brings you to the station this early in the morning?"

Rachel took a deep breath. "I've been thinking about what you said yesterday about being careful about the stories I write."

"Good. I'm glad you listened. I wouldn't want to see you get hurt."

"I don't either, but I have a job to do. I have to tell the stories of the gang killings and how their presence in the neighborhoods is a danger to the people there. This may mean I have to dig a little deeper into the gang culture. I thought you might be able to give me some pointers about how I should proceed."

Matt frowned and leaned forward. "These are dangerous people, Rachel. They don't appreciate attention. I'm not about to give you advice that might get you killed."

Rachel waved her hand in dismissal. "So far I haven't focused on them other than to report what the police have told me about the murders." She scooted to the edge of her chair. "But the facts are that at least six gang members have been murdered in the past few weeks. I'm beginning to wonder if there's more to the story."

Matt's hair tumbled across his forehead and he brushed at it. "What do you mean?"

She got up and closed the door. Returning to his desk, she planted her hands on the top and leaned forward. "I talked to a mother at that murder scene yesterday. She's scared for her son to leave the house. I feel a responsibility to the people who're living in the shadow of these bullies."

He jumped to his feet. "They're more than just bullies,

Rachel. They're dangerous. You need to stay away from them."

Rachel straightened and crossed her arms. "I'm not looking for trouble. I just need to know how to talk to them. You probably encounter them on a daily basis in your job, and I know you volunteer at the Youth Center. So you deal with the kids who live in the neighborhoods controlled by them."

Matt walked around the desk, stopped in front of her and shoved his hands in his pocket. The muscle in his jaw twitched. "I do. And I see what it does to their lives. They live in a violent world."

Rachel thought about the whispered words she'd heard the night before from someone wanting to escape that environment. To help him she needed to understand it. "That's why I came to you. I know all about the Center's success record with these inner-city kids. You can help me understand what it's like for them."

He pulled a hand from his pocket and raked it through his hair. With a sigh he returned to his chair. He sat in deep thought before he looked up. "I can't even imagine the terror they feel each night. Afraid that at any time a stray bullet could sail through their window and kill one of their family members like it did Carlos's baby brother last month. I was the detective who questioned the family after the shooting."

Rachel swallowed and eased into her chair. "That must have been difficult."

His eyes took on a faraway look. "Can you imagine what it's like to tell a mother there was no reason for her baby to die? Or to calm down a teenage brother when he's ranting that he's going to find whoever shot into their house and kill him? And all the while the mother's begging him to be quiet, she doesn't want to lose another son."

A bitter taste flowed into Rachel's mouth. "That must have been horrible."

"It was, but the sad thing is it only seems to be getting

worse. When morning comes, I don't know how the kids gather their courage and go to school where they know at least half the students are carrying concealed weapons." He took a deep breath before he continued, "How do children survive in such surroundings?"

The concern she saw in Matt's eyes pricked Rachel's heart. "These kids are lucky to have people like you who care."

Matt shook his head. "I don't know about that. I've been fighting the effects of these criminals ever since I came to Lake City five years ago, and I'm mystified by what I see. No matter how bad it gets, too many kids long to be like the guys who are destroying their neighborhoods. Wannabes, I call them. They hang around the fringe of the gangs just waiting until they're old enough to throw their lot in."

"Surely there are some success stories."

He leaned back in his chair and rubbed his hands over his eyes. "Yeah, there are some. I'd like to have more, though."

Guilt coursed through her. "David's asked me several times to volunteer at the Center but I've always put him off. Maybe it's time I did my duty and helped out more."

Matt smiled. "He'd like that. We can always use extra help."

Rachel nodded and stood. "I'll talk to him about it. This might help me to understand better what I've been writing about."

Matt walked around the desk, pulled her coat from the rack and held it for her. "The gang members tend to stay away from the Center, but there's one thing you need to remember. With them, it's all about respect. They see themselves as the most respected individuals in their neighborhood. If you ever come in contact with them, be courteous. They'll respond to you in the same way. They leave the Center alone because of the way David treats them." He chuckled. "He told me once that it's because a lot of them are kids he didn't save."

She turned to face Matt. "I'll remember everything you've said."

Concern flickered in his eyes again. "Remember what I told you yesterday. You need to be careful with your stories. I don't want to answer a call that you've been hurt."

The warmth of his voice flowed over her and her breath caught in her throat. "I will be. But you're the one out on the streets. You take care of yourself, too. Thanks for seeing me, Matt."

He stared at her for a moment before he backed away. "Drop by anytime, Rachel."

Rachel glanced at her watch. "I've gotta go. See you later."

With a wave, she headed into the hallway. Before she exited the building, she looked over her shoulder. Matt stood in his office doorway watching her. She was relieved they had gotten on the subject of her volunteering at the Youth Center. At least he hadn't seen how his warnings about the gangs scared her.

She wondered what he would say if he knew what she intended to do tonight. A chill raced up her spine at the thought. Dangerous or not, she had to find out if her source was telling the truth.

She glanced at her watch and swallowed. Rendezvous time was a little over twelve hours away. If she was lucky, she might have a good story. She chuckled and shook her head. No. In the words of her confidential source, she might have a story that would rock this city.

Matt's words of warning rang in Rachel's head as she pulled her car to the curb a little before midnight, turned off the motor and stared at the dark streets. Her skin prickled with fear. A city park one night and a slum the next. At least she was becoming familiar with new areas of the city.

She stepped from the car and started toward the meeting

place two blocks away. In the glow from a streetlight, she glanced at her watch. Eleven forty-five—fifteen minutes until showtime. She'd have to hurry if she was going to find a vantage point for watching. She pulled her coat tighter and hurried through the night.

Rounding the corner at Walters and Branson, she looked around for a hiding place. The stores still in business on the street were deserted, having closed hours ago and pulled iron gates across their fronts. Others sat like ghosts in the darkness with their doors and windows covered with boards.

Pondering which side would afford the best view, she crossed the street and walked several feet to a narrow alley that ran between two of the deserted stores. She flattened herself in the shadows against the brick exterior of one of the buildings and hoped that she was hidden from sight.

Her heart beat in her ears with a deafening thud. She pressed her hands to her chest and breathed deeply. No matter what happened, she had to keep control of her senses and observe every detail accurately.

The thumping in her chest slowed and she relaxed. Careful not to make a sound, she scrunched against the wall and waited.

From his position at the second-floor window of an abandoned building, he watched her slip into the alley across the street. "Well, Rachel Long. What are you doing here? If you're looking for a story, maybe I can oblige."

He had to hand it to her—she had spunk. Not many women would put themselves in danger by coming into this neighborhood at night, not even for the promise of a sensational story.

He picked up the sniper rifle lying beside him and stroked the weapon. Never had he seen a better barrel contour than this masterpiece exhibited.

He raised the rifle to his shoulder and peered through the

scope. Rachel's image came into his sights. It would be so simple. The paper might offer a reward for information leading to the arrest of the gang member who killed a crusading reporter.

His index finger hovered over the trigger. So simple.

The roar of an engine shattered his focus. He watched as a black sedan with tinted windows pulled to a stop, just over ten feet from Rachel.

He frowned as he studied the vehicle. He knew the owner, Terrence Cooper, well. Tonight was shaping up to be a fun-filled outing. Terrence might not think so if he knew what was about to happen.

Within moments, another car drove up and parked behind the sedan. A man jumped out and hurried toward Terrence's car. Even in the shadows he recognized Tom Carr.

A movement from the alley caught his attention and he swung the rifle to his shoulder. Evidently Rachel wanted a better view. He grasped the rifle tighter. The stock felt cool against his cheek and sent a thrill coursing through his body.

He peered through the scope at Rachel's magnified figure and then focused on the man on the sidewalk. Terrence, who had an envelope in his hand, emerged from the car and appeared in the scope's crosshairs. Three people who had no idea of the danger around them. He wavered back and forth. Who should be first? Tom reached for the envelope and stuffed it in his coat pocket.

There really was no choice. It was time for retribution. He held his breath and pulled the trigger.

THREE

The sharp crack of a rifle ricocheted off the brick buildings. Rachel slammed backward into the recesses of the alley. With the second shot, she fell to her knees and covered her head with her arms. Panting for breath, she waited for another report. When a third didn't follow, she pushed to her feet and inched toward the sidewalk.

The black sedan, its motor idling and its windshield shattered, hadn't moved. Beside it, a man with blood pouring from his head lay on the sidewalk. Another man sprawled next to him.

Afraid to expose her position, Rachel debated on whether or not to go to their aid. A third shot hit bricks on the front of the building. She screamed and jumped backward.

Yanking her cell phone from her pocket, she called 911.

The operator's voice crackled in her ear. "What is your emergency?"

"There's been a shooting at Walters and Branson. Two men are lying on the sidewalk and the shooter is firing at me."

"Help is on the way, ma'am. What's your position?"

"In an alley. Please tell them to hurry." She flipped the phone closed before the woman could ask more questions.

Footsteps pounded on the asphalt street. Rachel peeked out. A man sprinted from the shadows of a building across from her. Zigzagging as he ran, the shadowy figure headed toward the two lying next to the car.

Rachel's chest pounded with fear. Could he be the shooter? As if in answer to her question another shot rang out. The runner dived to the pavement behind the car as the bullet hit the back window.

Her chest heaved in panic as she looked around for an escape route. She took a step backward and her foot struck a tin can. As its clatter echoed in the alley, the man next to the bodies cocked his head to one side and pushed into a crouching position. His gaze locked on the alley.

Cold fear crept through Rachel's body. She had to get out of there. A streetlight burned at the far end of the alley. Willing her unresponsive body to move, Rachel turned and ran toward it as fast as she could. Behind her, footfalls echoed on the concrete.

"Police! Stop!"

The words registered in her mind, but the voice from behind only served as a command for her feet to move faster. How could the police have gotten here so quickly? It had to be the shooter chasing her. If she could get to the next street, maybe she could find a place to hide from him.

"I said stop!"

The light came closer and she pushed harder. Just a few more feet and she would—

Something blocked her path. Before she realized what was happening, she plowed into a rusted garbage can that sat in the middle of the alley.

She clawed at empty air as she fell forward. With a scream, she landed facedown on the hard concrete.

A hand clamped around her left arm and pulled. Pushing to her feet, Rachel straightened, whirled to face her pursuer and stared into the barrel of a gun. She shook free of the restraining hand. "Get away from me."

A loud gasp sounded and the hand released her arm. "Rachel?" The surprised croak bounced off the brick walls.

Shaking, she inched backward. Her attacker took a step forward into the light filtering into the alley. Rachel's knees almost buckled and she staggered even farther away.

She tried to speak but her vocal cords felt useless. She shook her head in denial. "Matt? What are you doing here?"

Matt blinked in disbelief and lowered the gun he held. He didn't know if he was more surprised at the two bodies lying on the pavement behind him or Rachel's presence at the scene of a murder. He rammed his revolver back in the holster and advanced on her with fists clenched.

Every expletive he'd ever heard came to mind. With a shake of his head he tried to banish old habits from the days before he turned his life over to God. Besides, if David had been right about Rachel's commitment to her job, nothing he said would faze her.

"What am I doing here? I'm a policeman doing my job. Do you realize you could've been killed?"

Her chin quivered. "I—I'm doing my job, too. I w-was following a lead for a story."

Matt leaned forward. He could smell the perfume he'd come to associate with her presence. The familiar reminder calmed his racing heart. "And did you just happen to pick this spot out of all the other streets in town?"

"No, of course not."

He pulled his cell phone from his pocket. "Tell me now, or so help me, I'll call your editor and tell him you've just interfered with a police stakeout. I don't think he'll like that too much."

At the end of the alley, police cruisers screeched to a stop and their blue lights bounced off the brick walls. Voices rang out as the officers converged on the shooting scene and shouted commands to search the buildings for the shooter.

Her shoulders slumped and she released a long breath. "All right. If you must know, there was a call to the office yesterday. The man said he wanted to meet with a reporter. We met last night and he told me there was a policeman taking payoffs from a Ranger. He said their meetings take place on this corner. I just wanted to see what I could find out."

His heart beat faster with each word she spoke. He raked his hand through his hair and stared at her. "You should've called me right away and told me about this. I warned you about the danger. Whoever shot these guys was shooting at you, too."

Even in the dim light he could see the fear that flashed in her eyes before she squared her shoulders and took a deep breath. "He was firing at you, too."

"His aim would've been better if he'd intended to hit me."

Rachel nodded. "He probably could have hit me, too, if he'd really wanted to kill me. Why do you think he did that?"

Matt shrugged. "Probably just wanted to scare us."

Sirens wailed in the distance. Matt took her by the shoulders. "Did you call the police?"

She nodded.

"Oh, great. Now we have other officers pulled off patrol to join the ones already here."

Her lips curled into a sneer. "Well, excuse me for trying to report a crime. I thought that was the right thing to do."

If she thought the mocking tone of her voice would anger him, she was wrong. He'd observed her fiery temperament and her competitive spirit at the other crime scenes. In fact, they were what had attracted him to her the first time he saw her. As much as he hated to admit it, she fascinated him.

"It was. But as I tried to tell you earlier today, I don't want you to end up dead right."

Several more police cars screeched to a halt at the entrance to the alley. Rachel tucked a strand of blond hair behind her ear, took a deep breath and hugged her purse against her body. "I suppose I'd better go talk to them."

Matt stepped aside and made a sweeping bow. "After you. I think it's time you met my partner."

Rachel hesitated a moment before she stepped from the alley. Several policemen were bending over the bodies. She could hear them talking but her mind was on Matt and how shocked she'd been when she stared at the gun pointed at her.

An unmarked police car stopped at the curb, and the man Rachel had seen with Matt at the shooting scene the day before climbed out. Matt led her over to where the man stood and stopped beside him. "Philip, this is Rachel Long, a reporter with the *Beacon*. Rachel, this is my partner, Detective Philip Nolan."

The man smiled and held out his hand. "I've seen Miss Long at some of the crime scenes before but we've never been introduced. It's good to finally meet you. I read all your stories. But how did the *Beacon* get a reporter down here so quickly?"

Matt glanced at Rachel. "Actually, she was here when it happened."

The detective pursed his lips and looked over at the bodies on the sidewalk. "Since Miss Long was here, why don't you get her statement and I'll talk to the first responders?"

Matt nodded, took her arm and led her down the sidewalk away from the bodies. "Now tell me about this call you got yesterday."

"I've told you all I know. I was just following the lead I was given."

Matt leaned against the brick front of a boarded up café. "Did you get a look at the informant?"

"No, he wouldn't let me turn around. He told me to refer to him as my confidential source." Rachel glanced up and down the street. "Where were you standing? I didn't see you until you ran to the car."

Matt pointed to a deserted building that had once housed a grocery store. "That doorway over there. I saw someone cross the street and go down the alley, but in the dark I didn't realize it was you. I thought it was one of the neighborhood residents taking a shortcut through the alley to the apartments on the next street. If I had recognized you, I would have gotten you out of here before anything happened."

She shook her head. "You couldn't have stopped me. I was determined to follow that lead. I just never expected to see two men killed." She glanced back at the crime scene. "Do you know who they are?"

"I can't release their names until their families have been notified."

Matt's reserved tone warned her that he didn't want to discuss the situation with her. Maybe her source had been right. If a policeman and a gang member had met for a scheduled payoff, someone had put a halt to their plans.

A cold wind blew down the street and Rachel pulled her coat tighter. "How long do you think I'll have to stay here?"

"You'll be able to leave soon."

Philip Nolan, who'd been talking with two of the crime scene investigators, turned and walked toward them. He stopped next to Matt and stared at Rachel.

"Miss Long?"

Her heart pounded as she nodded.

The man smiled and nodded in Matt's direction. "I know Matt has your statement but is there anything else you didn't tell him that might be important? We've got two dead bodies here, and we need something to help us find a killer."

Briefly, Rachel recounted the events of the previous night and continued until she ended with the arrival of the police at the shooting scene. "I never saw the shooter but I think he must have been in an upstairs window of one of the buildings across the street."

Matt's eyebrows arched. "That so? You didn't tell me that before."

She shrugged and pointed to a building across the street. "I just now thought of it. The sound seemed to come from that direction."

Reaching into his pocket, Philip handed her a card. "If you think of anything else, give us a call." He shoved the notepad in his pocket and turned to walk back toward the crime scene. Suddenly he stopped and spun around. "One more thing about this anonymous source. Be careful, Miss Long. I'd hate to see you get caught up in something dangerous."

Rachel smiled. "Matt's warned me about that. I thank you for your concern, also."

Philip studied her before he and Matt returned to the crime scene.

Rachel turned her back on the two bodies lying on the sidewalk and tried to direct her attention across the street to the building where she believed the killer had hidden. As she squinted into the distance, two uniformed policemen walked by.

The one nearer her looked at the other officer and shook his head. "I can't believe it. Tom Carr taking payoffs. He was almost ready to retire. Why would he get mixed up with a gang?"

The other man shook his head. "I don't know. Did you see the wad of money they pulled out of that envelope in his pocket? The press is going to have a field day with this. I can see the headlines now. Corrupt detective killed taking payoff from a gang member."

The men glanced at her as if seeing her for the first time, but she gave no indication she noticed them. Her mind raced with the information that confirmed what her source had said.

Her stakeout had paid off. She had the headline for tomorrow's newspaper.

Rachel straightened as Matt walked back to where she stood. "You can go now." He stared up the street. "Where's your car?"

Rachel pointed in the direction she'd parked. "About two blocks down."

Matt took her by the arm. "Mine's around the corner. Since I've got to go to the police station, I'll drive you to your car. Then I'm going to follow you home. Just want to make sure you get there safely."

The thought of walking back to her car, especially with a killer on the loose, had been niggling at the back of her mind ever since the shooting. Matt's suggestion put her mind at ease.

"Thanks. I'd appreciate that."

With a final wave at the officers, Matt steered her around the corner and down the block to where his police car was parked.

Several minutes later he stopped beside her vehicle. She turned to thank him but he was staring past her. "Oh, Rachel," he murmured.

She twisted in her seat to follow his gaze, and her eyes flared. "Wh-what happened?"

He shifted the car into Park and reached for the door handle. "It looks like you just got a welcome to the neighborhood."

Her legs felt like limp spaghetti as she climbed out and walked over to her car. The window on the driver's side had been broken, and the door stood slightly ajar. She could see the contents of the glove compartment scattered across the front seat. The case holding all her CDs was missing.

She glanced at Matt, who knelt beside one of the tires. He pushed to his feet and brushed his hands together. "All four tires are slashed and the hubcaps are gone."

Tears flooded her eyes as she gazed across the dented hood

and broken windshield. "It looks like they used a baseball bat on it."

He nodded. "Yeah, or something like that." He shook his head. "I'm sorry, Rachel, but this isn't unusual for this neighborhood."

She blinked the tears away and took a deep breath. "Well, you did warn me."

"Yeah, but being right doesn't make me feel any better."

A nearby streetlight lit his face. There was no mistaking the look of concern he directed at her. She pulled her cell phone from her pocket. "I guess I'd better call a tow truck to take my car to a garage."

"Would you like me to take care of that for you?"

Relief flowed through her. "Would you, Matt? I have to admit I don't have a clue who to call."

He laughed. "Then get back in the car and I'll call the guy we use at the station."

She scrambled back inside the police car and watched as Matt placed a call. After speaking for a few minutes, he nodded and ended the call. Opening the driver's side door, he climbed in and smiled. "No problem. He'll come get your car right away and take it to his shop on Cedar Street. You can talk to him in the morning."

"Thanks, Matt. I really appreciate that." She hesitated a moment. "And thank you for being concerned about my safety. You're a good friend."

He turned the ignition and cleared his throat. "Would you like for me to pick you up for work in the morning?"

She shook her head. "No, I'll call my insurance company and get a rental until my car is fixed. Although I wish I could junk the car."

He glanced at her and then back at the road. "What's wrong with it?"

"It's old and about ready to die. The only problem is I can't afford a new one yet. Maybe these stories will change that."

"How so?"

Rachel settled back in the seat and stared out the window. "My job at the *Beacon* is just a stopover on my way up the ladder of success. If I do a good job with these stories, maybe I'll get noticed by a TV station that needs an investigative reporter or a big-city newspaper. I'd settle for anything that pays more money than I'm making now."

When Matt didn't say anything, she glanced at him. His mouth had drawn into a grim line and he appeared to be concentrating on his driving. For the remainder of the trip he didn't speak except to ask directions. When they stopped at the entrance of her apartment building, she unbuckled her seat belt and turned to him.

"Thanks for everything tonight, Matt."

His fingers gripped the steering wheel. "Glad I could be of help." He hesitated a moment before he swallowed and licked at his lips. "There is one more thing, though."

"Another question about the shooting?"

"No, something else."

Matt turned to face her and his gaze flitted across her face. A ripple of pleasure coursed through her. She noticed for the first time the dark eyes that seemed to bore into her soul. Her cheeks warmed, but she couldn't break the contact with his gaze. Her breath caught in her throat.

"What is it?"

"I wanted to ask if you'd go with me to the Fox Theater Saturday night."

Rachel opened her mouth to say no, but she couldn't find the words. She'd passed the elegant old theater many times, but she'd never been able to afford a ticket for a performance. "The Fox Theater?"

Matt rubbed his hand around the steering wheel rim. "Well, you see, I have these two tickets to the Christmas production of *The Nutcracker* that the Lake City Ballet is doing and I don't want to go alone. It'd be nice if you could join me. We could grab a bite of dinner before and then go to the theater."

"Dinner and the ballet?"

What was the matter with her? She shouldn't even think about going. She'd promised herself nothing would interfere with her plans. Something warned her Matt could become a distraction. But what harm could one night cause?

"I'd love to go."

A big breath escaped his mouth. "Good. I'll call you later with a time."

"That will be fine."

He smiled and reached across her to open the door. "If you change your mind about a ride to work in the morning, let me know."

She smiled and stepped from the car. "I will."

Rachel watched until the taillights of Matt's car disappeared in the distance before she walked into the apartment building lobby. She breathed a sigh of relief to be back on familiar ground. When she'd left earlier, she had no idea what awaited her on that dark neighborhood street.

She'd gone expecting to see a policeman take a bribe or maybe a drug deal going down. Never in her wildest dreams would she have expected to see two men murdered. On top of that, she couldn't have guessed that Matt Franklin would chase her down an alley.

The most unbelievable of all, however, might have been her agreeing to a date with Matt. One date didn't mean anything. It wasn't like she intended to begin a romantic relationship with him. She had more sense than that. Romance was the last thing on her mind. She'd certainly told herself that enough times.

Loneliness washed over her and she bit down on her lip. Where did this feeling she didn't understand come from? No matter how hard she tried to ignore it, at times she couldn't. She might have trouble understanding her emotions, but tonight had made her positive about one thing—there was a vigilante in Lake City.

FOUR

Rachel set her cup of coffee on her office desk, dropped into the chair at her computer and unfolded the newspaper's morning edition she'd picked up when she entered the *Lake City Daily Beacon* lobby. Just as she thought, her story had claimed the headline spot this morning. It wasn't often that a decorated police officer was killed while taking an alleged—as she'd carefully worded it—payoff from a gang member.

She skimmed the story that she'd filed soon after returning home the night before and smiled. Her presence at the crime scene lent credibility to her hinted allegations. It was the question of whether or not a vigilante was stalking the streets of Lake City that she read with interest. Such a declaration couldn't help but get her noticed, and according to the messages in her in-box this morning, this was exactly what had happened with her readers. It shouldn't take long for others in the media to follow.

Lost in thought about her story, she jumped when a knock sounded at the open door to her office. She glanced up to see Matt and Philip Nolan standing in the hall.

Even with the tired lines around Matt's eyes, she had to admit he was just about the best-looking guy she'd met in a long time. There was something different about the image he projected and the other policemen she'd seen at the gang-related murder scenes. Although she knew little about his background, one thing she did know—he was comfortable with who he was. She liked that about him.

She smiled and stood. "Good morning. Come on in." They walked into her office and stopped in front of her desk. The serious expressions on their faces told her this wasn't a social visit. "What are you doing here so early?"

Matt's dark eyes flickered across her face before he pointed to the newspaper lying on her desk. "We read your story."

The barbed tone of his words told her he was less than pleased. She raised her chin and stared at him. "What did you think?"

Before Matt could answer, Philip spoke up, "Needless to say, we were a little concerned. Where did you get the idea a police officer was one of the victims at last night's shooting?"

She motioned to the chairs across from her desk and sat down. When the two detectives were settled, she leaned forward and crossed her arms on her desk. "I heard two police officers talking. Although they mentioned Detective Carr's name, I didn't reveal his identity. I had no idea if his family had been notified of his death. Once we've established that they know, I'll print it. The citizens of Lake City have a right to know if one of our trusted police officers is really a crook who takes bribes." She looked from Matt to Philip. "It may cause your department some problems, but that's not my concern."

Anger flashed on Matt's face and he started to speak. Philip laid a restraining hand on his arm. "We understand your position, Miss Long, and we're not asking you for preferential treatment. However, we're just now getting to the bottom of this. When we have proof of any wrongdoing, the Chief will hold a press conference."

Rachel smiled. "I'll be in the front row."

Matt leaned forward, his elbows on the chair arms and his

hands clasped in front of him. "We just want to make sure that you don't do anything that will hamper our investigation."

She stared into his somber eyes. "I have no intention of interfering with the police."

He didn't break eye contact with her. "Then you'll cooperate with us?"

"I've always done that."

Matt's eyebrow arched. "From the calls the station is getting this morning, I don't think our captain would agree with that."

"What do you mean?"

Philip leaned forward. His eyebrows pulled down over his hawklike nose. His dark eyes bored into her. "Your story about a vigilante in Lake City has upset a lot of citizens. The phone has rung all morning from people wanting to know what the police are going to do about it."

There was no mistaking the annoyance in Matt's and Philip's eyes. Rachel bit back the retort hovering on her lips and considered their point of view. They were the ones who risked their lives every day to keep the citizens of Lake City safe.

She took a deep breath and forced a smile. "There's no one in this town who respects the police more than I do. But you need to understand that the press has a responsibility to keep the people informed. I hope you catch this guy soon so I can write the ending to this story."

Matt smiled. "So does that mean you'll help us?"

"Of course."

"By telling us what you learn from your source?"

Rachel glanced from Matt to Philip, a frown on her face. "You know I can't reveal a confidential source."

Philip shook his head. "We have a duty to protect the citizens of this city. If your informant knows something that can help our investigation, we need to know what it is."

Matt's forehead wrinkled and he stared at her. "Don't make

the mistake of thinking you're capable of dealing with these people. They're dangerous, Rachel."

There was no avoiding the concern she saw in Matt's eyes. The memory of a bullet striking the bricks above her head the night before sent a tremor through her. Perhaps in her haste to get a story she hadn't been careful enough.

She nodded. "I know the gangs pose a threat to everybody around them. If my source calls again and he agrees that I can tell you what he tells me, I'll let you know."

Philip's mouth crooked into a smile. "Well, until that time, how about not staking out any lonely street corners by yourself?"

Rachel chuckled. "Okay."

Matt stood. "We don't want anything to happen to you, Rachel."

Rachel glanced from Matt to Philip. "I appreciate that."

Philip let out a big breath, pushed to his feet and extended his hand. "It was nice to see you again, Miss Long."

"Please call me Rachel." She smiled and grasped his hand but pulled away when his ring pressed into her finger. "Ouch."

Philip's eyes grew wide and he released her hand. "I'm sorry. Did my ring hurt your finger?"

She rubbed her hand and gaped at the gold ring Philip wore. "I've never seen such a beautiful ring. It must be a family heirloom."

Philip smiled and held it out for Rachel to get a better look at the unusual design. The gold ring featured two hands that encircled the finger and met in the front to hold a crown perched atop a heart. "It's been passed down in my family for generations. Originally it was given to my great-great-grandmother when she married. It was a symbol of the love and faithfulness that she was promised. It's made its way through the family and was given to my father. When he died, it passed to my brother."

Rachel frowned. "Then how did you get it?"

Philip gazed down at the ring for a moment before he replied. "My brother died. Since he wasn't married, he wanted me to have the ring."

The sadness that flickered in his eyes pricked Rachel's heart. "I'm sorry. That must have been hard for you. I have a sister and I don't know what I would do if she was taken from me."

He smiled and straightened his shoulders. "Then don't take the time you have with her for granted. You never know what tomorrow will bring."

Rachel glanced at Matt. His eyebrows drew down across his nose, and she wondered what he was thinking. Philip's smile wavered as he glanced at Matt. He backed away from Rachel and pulled his cell phone from his pocket.

"If you'll excuse me, I have a few calls to make. I'll meet you at the car, Matt."

With a nod in Rachel's direction he turned and headed out the door. When he'd disappeared from view, Rachel tilted her head and crossed her arms. "You look tired this morning, Matt. What time did you get home last night?"

He exhaled and rubbed the back of his neck. "I was at the station until three o'clock."

Rachel stepped closer. "Is there something else wrong? The look you gave me when I was talking with Philip struck me as odd."

He hesitated a moment before he spoke. "I've known you for several months now and you never told me you have a sister. You only met Philip last night and you felt comfortable talking about your family."

Rachel opened her mouth in surprise and then laughed. "I can't believe you said that. For your information, Mr. All-Business Policeman, I don't think we've had a personal conversation until last night. I know nothing about you or where you grew up." She let her gaze drift over him. "I can tell from the expensive clothes you wear that there's something different about you from any detective I've ever known." She inched forward and lowered her voice. "So, tell me, do you have deep, dark secrets you're keeping? For all I know, yours could be worse than a sister."

Matt's face turned crimson and he stuck his hands in his pockets. "I guess we don't know much about each other. Maybe we can take care of that when we go out Saturday night."

She smiled. "I'd like that."

He glanced over his shoulder. "Well, I guess I'd better find Philip. I have a feeling he didn't have any calls to make and just wanted to give me some time to talk with you. I told him I was taking you out this weekend."

"And I need to get back to work. See you later."

Rachel watched Matt walk out of her office before she returned to her desk. She picked up the pen lying on the desktop and tapped it on the surface. Even though she'd joked with Matt about him being different, there was an element of truth to it. It wasn't just his expensive clothes, but rather the ease with which he wore them.

He'd said their date Saturday night would give them the opportunity to know each other better. She wanted to know more about Matt, but that meant opening up about her background, too. What would he say when he found out about her family? Probably what every other man she'd ever dated said. If so, she'd better enjoy Saturday night because there wouldn't be a second date.

In high school, the boys she'd grown up with were content to be friends at school, but not one of them had ever asked her on a date. Not even to prom. She'd made all kinds of excuses to her mother to cover her disappointment—there wasn't anybody she wanted to go with, spending money on a prom dress was ridiculous, she needed to study for finals.

But her excuses thudded like a hammer against her hollow heart.

College offered a fresh start with people who didn't know her. She'd fallen in love for the first time, and it had been perfect. Until she took her boyfriend, Justin, home to meet her family. She had thought he was different, that he would be able to accept her sister Cara and her disabilities, but she'd been wrong.

Cara's attempts to be friendly with Justin had been met with cold indifference. He wasted no time in telling Rachel that he'd never been comfortable around special-needs individuals and that he wouldn't have come if he'd realized how bad Cara's condition was. It came as no surprise when he ended their relationship a week later.

The worst blow had come, however, when she realized he'd warned all the guys he knew to keep their distance. She often wondered what stories he had told about his visit to her home, but she thought it better that she not know. She didn't need to add more anger to what she already felt over the hurt her mother and sister had suffered. They didn't deserve it. That experience did, however, confirm one thing for her. Love and marriage didn't have a place in her future.

The ringing of her telephone interrupted her thoughts and she reached for the receiver. "Rachel Long."

"I seen the morning paper."

Rachel's eyes widened at the sound of the familiar voice. She sat up straight. "You did?"

The man didn't speak for a moment. "So the vigilante got Terrence. He been with the Rangers a long time. Never met that cop but I heard the brothers talkin' 'bout him."

Rachel closed her eyes as the memory of what she'd seen the night before swept over her. "I've never seen anyone killed before."

"So, now you believe me?"

"Yes."

"Good. Then maybe we can help each other."

Rachel reached for a pen and paper. "Do you have anything else you can tell me?"

"Yeah. Can you meet me again?"

Rachel's heart raced. "Where?"

"Tonight. Same place, same time. How's that for you?"

Her fingers tightened around the pen. "I'll be there."

"I'll see you then."

"Wait," Rachel cried out. "Let me give you my cell phone number. You might need it sometime."

She recited the number and waited for a response. "Got it. See you tonight."

Silence on the other end told her the caller had disconnected. She hung up the phone and sank down in her chair. Her conversation with Matt and Philip replayed in her mind. They wanted her to let them know if her source called again. She reached for the phone, but then she drew her hand back.

Common sense told her she didn't need to go to this meeting alone, especially after what had happened last night. But the rendezvous time was over twelve hours away. She could decide later what she needed to do. With a sigh she swiveled her chair so she faced the computer. There were a lot of emails, and she wanted to see what the citizens of Lake City thought about a vigilante in their midst.

Three hours later, Rachel pulled on her coat and walked out of her office toward the elevator at the other end of the hall. She'd just pushed the down button when the elevator doors opened and her editor, Cal Belmont, stepped out.

His smile broadened when he saw her. "Good job on your story, Rachel. I've had a lot of emails this morning about a vigilante in Lake City."

"Thanks, Cal."

A man stepped around Rachel and moved into the elevator. She watched the door close and groaned inwardly. A conversation with her long-winded editor could turn into a lengthy chat, and her stomach was already rumbling the message that it was time for lunch.

Cal's glasses rested in the mass of gray curls on top of his head. He pulled them off and thumped them on the newspaper he held. "Great job, Rachel. We had the story before anybody. You never did tell me how you got it so fast."

"I got a tip that something was going down on that street corner. I thought I'd stake it out." She shrugged. "I guess it was a matter of being in the right place at the right time."

"Well, keep up the good work, but not so much that the competition wants to steal you from the *Beacon*."

Rachel reached around Cal and pushed the down button again. "I'm glad you appreciate my work." The doors slid open and Rachel stepped in before Cal could respond. "I'm on my way to lunch. See you later."

She smiled and punched the button for the lobby. Cal waved and turned away as the doors closed. Rachel breathed a sigh of relief to have sidestepped Cal's questions. With Matt and Philip concerned about her source, she didn't need to add Cal to the list.

When the elevator reached the lobby, she stepped to the double front doors and peered outside. The weather forecast for the day had mentioned a chance of snow.

A woman stopped outside and pushed the front door open. As Rachel moved out of the way for her to enter, she glanced over her shoulder. Across the lobby, a young man leaned against the wall, his stare directed at her. The heavy down jacket he wore looked like many others she'd seen, but it was the bulk of his chest and arms underneath that caught her attention. A wool knit cap covered his head, hiding his hair.

She'd never seen him in the building before. As his gaze met hers, he pushed away from the wall and took a step toward her.

Fear rushed through Rachel's body and she backed toward

the door. She could see his face better now. She was positive she'd never seen him before. He stuck his hand in his coat pocket as he advanced toward her. Her throat went dry. Was he reaching for something inside? A gun?

Rachel turned and bolted through the front door. The parking lot at the side of the building where she'd left her rental car this morning looked as if it were a mile away. She glanced over her shoulder. The man had followed her onto the sidewalk. He took a step in her direction before he halted, turned and ran across the street.

Rachel slowed her step and watched him climb into a red car. She had no idea the make of the automobile, so she concentrated on trying to remember how it looked. A dent creased the back fender and patches of chipped paint covered the trunk. The motor roared to life and the wheels squealed as the car shot into traffic.

Rachel breathed a sigh of relief and shook her head. She had to quit thinking about the bullet striking the bricks above her head and the two dead bodies on the street last night. If she didn't, she'd end up suspecting everyone she came in contact with was out to kill her.

A bell clanged and Rachel whirled in the direction of the parking lot. A Santa Claus, the bell in his hand pealing out a familiar holiday sound, stood at the corner, his kettle ready for donations from passersby. The reminder of a time-honored Christmas tradition calmed the fear she'd experienced a few minutes earlier. Since she was a child, she'd looked forward to seeing the Santas who dotted the streets of Lake City each December—their mission to see underprivileged children have a happy holiday.

Inhaling the cold air, she smiled and strode forward. The memory of how her mother struggled to provide a good Christmas for her two daughters had caused her to vow she would never pass a Santa's kettle without dropping in some money.

A vigilante and murders across the city weren't going to take away her yuletide spirit.

She stopped in front of the Santa and tried to suppress a smile. He wasn't as chubby as others she'd seen in the past, but that didn't matter. It was the size of one's heart that really described a person. To her way of thinking, anyone who would dress up in a Santa suit and stand on a street ringing a bell for donations had to have a heart the size of the whole state.

She grasped the strap of her purse and pulled it from her shoulder. "Let me get some money for you."

The Santa adjusted his beard, bent down and set his bell on the sidewalk. "Thank you."

Rachel grasped the bag in both hands and unzipped the purse. "I'm glad to help—"

Before she could finish her sentence, the Santa grabbed her purse and pulled it from her hands. Clutching it tightly, he bolted across the street.

Speechless, Rachel gaped at the disappearing figure in the fur-trimmed red suit running as if his life depended on it. After a few seconds she regained her senses enough to realize she'd just been the victim of a robbery. She dashed into the street in pursuit and yelled at the top of her lungs. "Stop! Thief!"

A car horn honked and brakes squealed. Rachel glanced around to see a delivery truck bearing down on her. She jumped backward and groaned when the vehicle blocked her view of the retreating figure. When it passed, the Santa had disappeared.

The despair she felt at having been robbed turned to anger. In the last two days she had been brought face-to-face with crime in Lake City. Maybe a purse snatching didn't rank as high as murder on the worst crime scale, but she felt violated.

She mentally listed the contents of her purse—a wallet containing thirty dollars, a credit card that was almost maxed out, her driver's license, cell phone, a necklace her mother had given her and makeup. The only thing she couldn't replace was the necklace, which had been a gift when she graduated college. She'd intended to get the clasp repaired today.

Rachel clenched her fists and gritted her teeth. How could she have been so careless? But then who would ever suspect Santa Claus of being a thief? She hoped he had a good time with her few possessions.

With a sigh she turned back to the newspaper office. She had to make a report to the police. Even if she never saw her purse again, she didn't want other people in Lake City to be robbed by a thief posing as Kriss Kringle.

She stopped before she entered the building and thought of Matt. What would he say? The memory of his words earlier returned, and an uneasy feeling crept over her. Maybe she should tell him about her meeting with the source tonight. Her instincts told her she could trust the person she'd met with and talked to on the phone. On the other hand, she thought she could trust Santa Claus and she'd been wrong about that.

Rachel straightened her shoulders and walked to the elevator. She knew what she had to do. Getting a story that would boost one up the ladder to success didn't mean a thing if you were dead. She was going to call Matt and tell him about her next meeting with the source.

He entered his apartment and dropped the sack containing the Santa Claus suit on the floor. When he'd run back to his car, it had only taken a minute to discard the outfit and stuff it in the sack before he drove away. It was a good thing he knew the neighborhood around the *Beacon* building. He'd had the perfect spot to park his car and change clothes undetected.

With a smile he spread the morning newspaper on the kitchen table and dumped the contents of Rachel Long's purse on it. He chuckled at the assortment of articles that tumbled out. There were the items you'd expect to find in any woman's purse—wallet, keys, makeup. But the other things told the story of the woman who had written about him in the morning edition.

For a moment his hatred for Rachel flashed through him like a raging fire. She'd called him a vigilante, a rogue killer who endangered everyone by his disregard for the law. He laughed. The only law he lived by was an eye for an eye. Why couldn't she see the service he was doing the citizens of Lake City by taking criminals off the street?

He took a deep breath and willed his heart to resume its normal beat. He couldn't let his dislike for the *Beacon's* hotshot investigative reporter overshadow his goal. There was too much at stake. He'd take care of her when the time was right.

He directed his attention back to the items from her purse. A sterling silver cross on a chain caught his eye, and he held it up. Stones he assumed to be diamonds covered the surface of the cross. A close examination revealed that the clasp was broken.

"Oh, too bad, Miss Long." He laid the necklace at the edge of the table. "I'll put this away for safekeeping. It might come in handy later on."

He picked up a receipt from a supermarket and glanced down the list of items she'd purchased. Yogurt, cereal, bananas, coffee. Breakfast items for someone on the go. Receipts from restaurants told him she didn't cook much at home.

Several envelopes lay on top of the pile of items and he picked them up. One contained her November paycheck stub. He smiled at her salary. She wasn't getting rich but she made enough to live comfortably.

The deductions caught his eye and he frowned. Over half her paycheck had been deposited into a savings account. She was paying all her bills and living on only half of her income. He wondered what that was all about. Maybe he could find the answer to his question.

He smiled and picked up her cell phone. It seemed only a few years ago that cell phones were unheard of. Now they were a link to everything and everybody in a person's life. And Rachel's phone was about to give him the answers he needed to put an end to the nosy reporter.

He reached for a box on the kitchen cabinet and sat down at the table. Opening the box, he read the instructions. When he'd finished, he picked up Rachel's cell phone and began the process of downloading spyware to her phone. When he was finished, he would have access to every conversation, text and email she received or sent.

There were still a few details he had to take care of before the fun could begin. He had to toss the purse in a Dumpster and then call the police to report seeing a Santa Claus throwing a woman's bag into the garbage bin. After that, he'd know every move Rachel Long made.

She had no idea what was about to happen to her.

FIVE

Matt Franklin swallowed the last bite of his hamburger and washed it down with a soft drink. Eating lunch at his desk was getting to be a habit, but he didn't mind. He'd never cared much for joining the guys on the force at the crowded diner down the street from the station. He always felt out of place with all the good-natured laughter and joking that went on with his colleagues.

That feeling of insecurity probably came from all the time he spent alone growing up. He'd just never learned to fit in. Quiet times—like candlelit dinners and walks along the lakeshore—appealed to him more. He wondered if Rachel Long enjoyed things like that. He kept telling himself not to get his hopes up too high about their date on Saturday night but he couldn't help it.

From the first time he'd seen her, there was something about her that drew him to her. And yet he was afraid to get better acquainted. He'd been disappointed too many times before.

One of the things he liked about Rachel was that she had a reserved quality about her that made him want to know her better. She accepted him as just another police officer she'd met at crime scenes and never plied him with questions about his personal life. Most women he'd known in the past weren't like that. Their main interests centered on his family.

He'd been a little uncomfortable this morning when Rachel had mentioned her family to Philip. Although he dreaded telling her about his, he really wanted to know more about what it was like for her growing up.

The ring of the phone on his desk interrupted his thoughts. "Detective Matt Franklin. May I help you?"

"Matt, this is Rachel."

His heartbeat quickened at the sound of her voice. "Rachel, to what do I owe the pleasure of a call from you?"

A long sigh echoed in his ear. "I wanted you to know I've learned two things today."

Puzzled, he frowned. "And what would those be?"

"Well, for one I've learned what a BOLO means."

His frown turned into a grin. "That's what the police use now instead of APB, all-points bulletin."

"I know."

"And what does a 'be on the lookout' have to do with what else you've learned?"

"Because the second thing I know is that you can't trust Santa Claus. The police have a BOLO out for him."

He sat up straight and gripped the phone tighter. "Rachel, what are you talking about?"

Matt listened as she told him about the purse snatching. "I've reported the incident to the police, but I wanted you to know that today isn't much better than last night. There is one good thing, though. At least Santa didn't shoot at me."

Matt shook his head. "I don't like this, Rachel. There are too many things happening to you at once."

"But I don't think the two could be related. I can't imagine a Ranger or a Viper dressing up like Santa just to steal my purse. And why would the sniper want it? If he wanted to do something to me, he could have shot me last night."

"Still, it could be related." He paused a moment. "Maybe patrol can spot something this afternoon. I'll check on it and let you know if they find anything."

"Thanks, Matt. I appreciate that. Also there's one more thing I need to tell you."

"What's that?"

"My source called again right after you and Philip left."

"And?"

"He wants me to meet him again tonight."

"Did you tell him that Philip and I want to meet him?"

"No, but I wanted to tell you because after all that's happened I'm not sure I want to go to that meeting alone."

Matt nodded. "That's a wise decision. Do you want us to go with you?"

"I'm afraid we might scare him off if too many people show up. I want you to go with me and stay in the car in case I need help. Will you agree to that?"

Matt pondered the question and saw the logic of not having two policemen accompany a reporter into the park. "Okay, but I don't feel right about not telling Philip."

"This may be our only chance to get more information from my source. If I go out there with two policemen and he finds out, I may lose him as a source and he'll lose his chance for a better life. You can explain this to Philip later."

Matt sighed. "Okay, Rachel. I'll do it. And I'll check on your purse this afternoon."

"Thanks, Matt. I had the keys to the rental car in there, so I've called for another set."

"Do you need me to pick them up for you?"

"No, thanks, they'll bring them to me. And thanks for understanding about the source. Can you meet me in the *Beacon* parking lot about ten o'clock tonight?"

"I can do that. I'll see you then."

"Bye."

Matt hung up the phone and shook his head. Why hadn't he asked her to have dinner with him first? He'd been thinking about how he wanted to get to know her better right before she called, and he had just passed up an opportunity to spend some time with her.

Maybe his college buddies had been right about him. He shied away from women because he feared he would learn some things about them he didn't like. In his heart he knew no one was perfect, and he wasn't looking for perfection. All he wanted was a woman whose eyes he could stare into and see love shining there for him instead of the flashing dollar signs he'd encountered in every other woman he'd ever known.

He dreaded telling Rachel about his wealthy family. No matter how hard he'd tried to distance himself from all the trappings of his mother's jet-set life, it had ruined every relationship he'd ever had. Maybe Rachel would look at him as an ordinary man dedicated to police work instead of the wealthy son from a family who traveled in an elite social circle.

He wanted to believe it but he didn't know for sure. Only time would tell.

Rachel glanced at her watch. She'd been so busy all afternoon that the time had just slipped away. It was nearly five o'clock. She reached to turn off her computer but stopped when someone knocked on her closed office door.

"Come on in."

The door swung open and her eyes grew wide. Matt stood in the doorway holding her purse toward her. A smile curled his lips. "Did you lose something?"

She jumped up and ran to him. "Where did you find it?"

He stepped into her office, grinned and held the bag out to her. "As much as I'd like to take credit for some good detective work, I can't. We received a call at the station this afternoon. The caller said he'd just seen a Santa Claus toss a woman's purse into the Dumpster in back of Taylor's Automotives. A patrol officer went over there and found your purse inside."

She took the purse from him and clutched it to her body. "Thanks for bringing it over."

He inclined his head toward her. "You'd better check it out and see what's missing."

"Okay." She hurried back to her chair behind her desk and opened the purse.

Matt slid into the chair across from her. "We kept a list of everything we found inside. We need you to tell us what was stolen."

Rachel did a quick inventory and glanced up at Matt. "My cash is gone, but it was only about thirty dollars. My credit card is missing, but I called and reported it stolen this afternoon. Thank goodness my cell phone and driver's license are here. The only other thing I can't find is the necklace my mother gave me when I graduated from college. The clasp was broken and I was going to take it to the jeweler on my lunch hour. I sure do hate to lose that."

Matt nodded. "What does it look like?"

"It's a sterling silver cross set with diamonds and hangs on an eighteen-inch chain. It always reminded me of my mother and sister. I'll miss not having it around my neck."

Sadness flickered in Matt's eyes. "I'm sorry. I'll put out a description to all the pawnshops in town. We might get lucky and be able to return it to you."

Rachel smiled. "I appreciate that. My sister, Cara, will be so upset when she finds out it was stolen."

"Is it an expensive necklace?"

Rachel shook her head. "Not really. It's the sentiment behind it that makes it special. Every time Cara saw it she would tell everybody that it was a sign that I went to college. I suppose it was special to her because deep in her heart she realized she could never do that."

Matt tilted his head and frowned. "Your sister couldn't go to college? Why?"

Rachel took a deep breath and wondered how Matt would respond when she told him. "Well, you see, she couldn't go because Cara has mental and physical disabilities."

Matt's eyes grew large. "She's a mentally challenged child?"

Rachel laughed. "Yes, but she's not a child anymore. She's ten years younger than I am, but she's my best friend."

"It must be nice having a sister. I'm an only child."

Rachel took a deep breath and stood. "I have to admit, when I was younger I sometimes wished I could be an only child, but I wouldn't give up Cara for anything."

Matt's solemn stare made her wonder what he thought about the revelation about her sister. If he was anything like the guys she'd known in the past, he would find some excuse to hurry off. She waited for him to rise and tell her something had come up and he wouldn't be able to take her to the ballet Saturday night.

Matt stared at her a moment longer before he glanced at his watch. "I didn't know it was getting so late. Are you hungry? We could go grab something to eat before it's time to meet your source. How about it?"

Rachel's heart soared. "I'd like that."

He glanced at his watch. "I need to go back to the station and finish up some loose ends there. How about we meet in an hour?"

A chime from Rachel's computer alerted her that an email had just arrived. She frowned. "That's from my editor. He always finds something else for me to do just before it's time for me to leave. Let me see what he wants. This may take some time."

Matt pulled a notepad and pen from his pocket, scribbled something on it and pushed the paper across her desk. "This is my cell phone number. Call me when you get ready to leave and I'll meet you in front of the police station." He hesitated. "That is, unless you'd prefer I drive."

She laughed and stood up. "It's the least I can do. Especially since I've protested so much about this being my story."

"Okay, I'll see you later."

Her stomach fluttered when he flashed a smile at her, and she clasped her hands in front of her in an effort to stop the trembling. What was the matter with her? She hadn't been affected like that since she had her first crush in high school.

When Matt walked from the office, she sank down in her chair, rested her elbows on the desktop and covered her face with her hands. Her skin warmed at the memory of Matt's smile. She'd told Matt earlier today that she'd learned two things. Now she had to admit she'd made a third discovery. If she didn't watch out, she could become interested in Matt. She had to make sure that didn't happen.

Matt finished the paperwork on a case he and Philip had closed earlier and laid the folder aside. Across the small office, Philip glanced up from his desk where he was studying the reports on the shooting deaths the night before.

Philip rubbed his eyes and stood up. "I just don't understand it. How could a good cop like Tom Carr get involved with the gangs?"

Matt shrugged. "I don't know, but we've seen it happen before. An officer gets closer to retirement and he begins to think how little he's going to be drawing. So he decides he has to make some quick money. Unfortunately, taking bribes to look the other way can be mighty tempting."

Philip nodded. "I guess so, but it sure didn't pay off for Tom. He's dead and his family has to deal with the fact that he died a criminal just like the ones he arrested for years. It's sad."

Matt thought of Tom's wife, who was a member of his church, and guilt flowed through him. "I need to go see Janine, but I thought I'd give her some time. I heard the funeral is going to be a private one. And there isn't going to be a wake."

"Maybe we can visit her together in a day or two after the funeral."

"That sounds good. We'll plan on that."

Philip reached for his jacket that hung on the back of his chair. "I think I'll go on home. It's been a long day."

Matt thought of the long night ahead and sighed. "Yeah. Have a good night."

Philip waved as he headed out the door. "See you tomorrow."

Matt glanced at his watch and wondered why Rachel hadn't called. It had been over an hour since he'd arrived back at the office. He'd no sooner had the thought than his cell phone rang.

He pulled the phone to his ear. "Hello."

"Hi, Matt. This is Rachel. I'm on my way to the newspaper parking lot and should be at the station in about fifteen minutes."

"Look, Rachel, are you sure you want to go through with this? I still don't feel good about you meeting this guy alone. I think I should be the one to talk to him."

"Oh, no." A small groan came over the line and he frowned.

"What's the matter?"

"Nothing. I was having trouble getting the door of the rental car to unlock. I'll be glad to get my car back, but the garage said it could be several weeks. Anyway, to answer your question, yes, I want to go through with this. We decided that I would talk to him and you would wait in the car. There's no need to change things now."

"All right, but I may try to convince you differently at dinner. Hurry up. I'm starving."

She laughed and a thrill raced through him. "See you in a few minutes."

He ended the call and stood by his desk thinking how Rachel had looked the first time he'd met her at a murder

ne. She hadn't been wearing a hat that day and the wind
d blown her blond hair about her face. When she tucked a
strand behind her ear, he gazed into the most beautiful blue
yes he'd ever seen. She had smiled and he hadn't been able
to get her out of his mind since.

It had been a long time since he'd met a woman that interested him like Rachel did and even longer since he'd had dinner with anyone as beautiful. This might not be a regular date. It was their work that had brought about their meeting. He would try to put the meeting out of his mind during dinner because the thought of gangs and murder wasn't going to keep him from enjoying her company tonight.

Matt drained the last drop of coffee from his cup and set it back in the saucer. In spite of his earlier resolve, he couldn't get his mind off the encounter with her source that would come later.

"You're sure you don't want me to go with you to the park bench to meet your source?"

Rachel frowned and set her fork down on her plate. "Do we have to go over this again? I've explained it to you. We don't need to scare him off. You'll be close enough that I'll call if I need you."

Matt pushed his plate out of the way, leaned forward and crossed his arms on the tabletop. "I want to make sure that you're safe." He grinned. "I don't want to read a headline that says a reporter was shot while a policeman hid behind a tree."

"You don't have to worry about that. My source sounds young to me. Of course, I don't know how young, but he doesn't strike me as being violent."

Matt's eyebrows arched and he laughed. "He's in a gang, Rachel. Of course he's violent."

She shook her head. "But he said he's a believer. He wants to please his mother by getting out of the gang life while he

can. He's asked me to help him get out of the city and I
going to do it."

"And just how are you going to accomplish that?"

"I'll talk to David. He has contacts all over the country
Maybe a director of another center can find a temporary home
for him away from the streets of Lake City."

There was no denying the sincerity in Rachel's voice. She
really did want to help this boy. "So he's more to you than a
story."

She settled back in her chair. "Of course he is. I don't want
to see him hurt. But I do want to tell his story." Her brow
wrinkled. "No, it's more that that. I've *got* to tell his story."

A subtle change had come over Rachel and Matt didn't
understand what had happened. "What do you mean?"

"I realize you don't know very much about me, Matt, but
one thing you need to understand is that my job at the *Beacon*
is temporary."

He sat up straight, his eyes wide. "Temporary? Have you
taken another job somewhere else?"

She shook her head. "No, but I plan to. I want to advance
to something bigger. An investigative reporter for a big TV
station. Something that pays more money than what I make
here."

Disappointment surged through him. "You said something
about that the other night. Now it sounds more like an obses-
sion. Are you saying that money is important to you?"

Rachel nodded. "A job that pays me a lot is important to
me."

Matt swallowed and searched for something to say but his
mind was blank. He still didn't understand fully what she'd
said. It wasn't a bad thing to want to advance in your career
and be paid for your work, but something in her eyes told him
it was more that just getting a better job.

She'd never struck him as a girl whose head could be
swayed by money, but that's what he'd thought before and

been proven wrong. Their date Saturday night should be an opportunity for his questions about Rachel to be answered. Until then they had other things to worry about, like a confidential source and a vigilante on a killing spree.

SIX

Rachel pulled her rental car into the same parking space she'd used two nights before and glanced at the trees behind the picnic area. Her source could be watching from there. Beside her, Matt remained silent as he had done ever since they left the restaurant.

"It's almost midnight. I need to get going."

Matt turned and grasped her arm. "Be careful, Rachel. If anything goes wrong, you scream as loud as you can and I'll come running."

She nodded and stepped from the car. As she walked toward the bench where she'd sat before, she wondered if tonight the mysterious source would tell her his name.

Rachel approached the picnic area and eased onto the park bench. The night air chilled her and she huddled in her coat to keep warm. The minutes dragged by but no one appeared. Rachel crossed her legs and scooted back farther on the seat. The low moan of the wind rustling the bare tree branches struck her taut nerves like a hammer against an anvil.

She gripped the edge of the seat and held on in defiance of the misgivings flowing through her. It was only a few minutes past midnight. A few more minutes. She could wait that long. He'd be here.

A hand clamped on her shoulder, sending shock waves through her body. "Sorry I'm late."

The mellow tones of his voice calmed her racing heart. The need to put a face to the voice overcame her but she didn't dare budge. She'd come for information and she couldn't scare him away.

"I thought you weren't coming. I was afraid your brothers found out about your meeting with me."

"Naw, they don't know nothin'. Fact is they too busy talkin' about the killin' last night."

Rachel nodded. "I can imagine."

"Yeah, they really upset. They say the Rangers gonna blame us now for what happened to Terrence and that cop. You was there. You think we done it?"

She closed her eyes and relived the panic she'd felt when a bullet hit the bricks above her head. "No. I believe you're right. I think there's a vigilante."

"And what makes you think that?"

"Whoever killed those men had to be an excellent marksman. He was well hidden and he hit his targets with two rapid shots. Since most of the gang members are kids recruited off the streets, I doubt there's one who could do that. Besides, you said a gang member would want to be up close to show their colors."

His hand struck the back of the bench. "Why can't the popo see that? Why they gotta waste time blaming us when they should be lookin' for the killer?"

Rachel shook her head. "I don't know. I just can't figure out what to do next."

"Maybe I can." His voice sounded closer. Her insides quaked like gelatin but she didn't look around. "The Rangers sent us word they read your story and think you may be right about a vigilante. They want to set up a meetin' to talk 'bout a truce until the popo catch this dude. Some of the brothers believe them, some don't. Big T, our leader, say we gonna try. So he's going tomorrow night to talk to Franco from the Rangers."

"Do you know where they're meeting?"

"Pepper's Bar on Locust Street."

Rachel swallowed back the uneasy feeling pushing its way up from her stomach. "That's near Randolph, isn't it?"

"Yeah. Why?"

"I was just thinking that's near where your friend was killed the night you were with him. If the Rangers wanted to meet, why wouldn't they choose neutral territory? Why come to the Vipers' turf?"

The man chuckled. "That's what I'm thinking. Sounds kind of like a setup, don't it?"

Rachel tried to smile but her trembling lips wouldn't obey. She took a deep breath. "Okay, I guess I'll have to check this out. What time are they supposed to meet?"

"Eleven o'clock. The manager's gonna close up and let them have the place to themselves."

Rachel nodded. "Thanks for the information. When will I hear from you again?"

Only silence greeted her question.

"Are you there?"

No answer.

She counted to ten before she turned around. No one stood behind her. If he was watching her from the forest behind, the trees guarded his whereabouts. She clutched her purse against her body, jumped up from the bench and ran as fast as she could toward her car.

The car sat alone in the parking lot underneath a streetlight. The thought of Matt waiting inside spurred her to run, and she raced toward safety. Rachel mentally counted the steps as her feet skimmed the surface of the asphalt—ten, eleven, twelve, thirteen.

Just a few more steps and she'd be with Matt. Fourteen, fifteen, sixteen. With a sigh of relief she reached out, grabbed the door handle and tugged.

Her heart pounded in her ears and a scream froze in her throat as strong fingers wrapped around her wrist.

Rachel clenched her fist and whirled to strike at her attacker. Then she sagged against the car in relief. "Matt, what are you doing? You were supposed to stay in the car."

He released her arm. "I know, but I got worried about you. You've been gone too long."

Rachel placed her hand on her chest and felt the thump of her heart through her coat. "He was late." She glanced past Matt and frowned. "But where were you? I didn't see you near us."

"I stayed in the trees. I couldn't get close enough to see his face. He was wearing a coat with a hood that hid most of his body." He chuckled under his breath. "I'm sorry I scared you. When I saw you running back to the car, I thought something had happened."

She shook her head. "No, I was in a hurry because I was cold."

In the beam from the streetlight, she watched a skeptical look spread across Matt's face. "And you sure you weren't a little frightened?"

Rachel started to deny it but she knew it was no use. She straightened her shoulders and raised her chin. "Well, maybe a little, but I thought there was a policeman waiting in my car to protect me."

He laughed. "Don't worry. I had your back." He pointed to the car. "Do you want me to drive?"

"No, thank you. I'm quite able to drive, even if you did scare the life out of me."

She climbed into the car and waited for Matt to get in the passenger seat. When he was settled, he buckled his seat belt and glanced at her. "Well, are you going to tell me what happened?"

As she guided the car into the street, she related what had taken place at the park bench and waited for his reaction. He stared ahead through the windshield, a thoughtful expression on his face.

She took a deep breath. "So, what do we need to do about tomorrow night?"

He directed a wide-eyed stare at her. "What do you mean we? This is a matter for the police."

She shook her head. "Why? My source said they were going to meet to talk. That's not against the law. What would you tell the police—that there are gang members sitting together in a bar? No. I think it would be better if we checked this out ourselves."

Matt sat silent for a moment before he responded, "I see your point. If anything happens, I can call for backup." He swiveled in his seat to face her. "But there's no need for you to be there."

She gripped the steering wheel tighter. "Oh, yes there is. This is my story and you're not going to cheat me out of it. You wouldn't even know about the meeting if it wasn't for me."

He sighed. "Okay, have it your way. We'll stake out the bar together."

She smiled. "I'm glad you see it my way."

"As if I had a choice. If I said no, you'd just show up anyway. At least this way I can keep an eye on you."

Rachel smiled and concentrated on her driving. Matt didn't speak again until they arrived at the police station. When she stopped, he climbed from the car and bent over to peer inside at her. "Thanks for driving. I'll talk to you tomorrow."

"That sounds good."

Rachel watched Matt disappear around the corner of the building before she pulled away from the curb and drove toward home. Her thoughts drifted to the Santa Claus who'd stolen her purse. So far there had been no other victims of a rogue Santa in Lake City. Even though she thought it unlikely, she couldn't help but wonder if the incident had something to do with her stories about the gangs.

Goose bumps raced up her arms at a sudden thought. Whoever took her purse now knew where she lived from the information on her driver's license. Could it be possible that the Santa was the vigilante? If so, maybe she needed to take Matt's concerns more seriously.

Matt pulled into his assigned parking space at the police station and turned off the ignition. His cell phone lay on the seat next to him and he stared at it, unsure of what to do. He remembered the flash of fear he'd seen in Rachel's eyes the night before when he grasped her wrist. At that moment, a protective feeling had swept through him and he had wanted to tell her she could depend on him to take care of her. Instead he'd masked his feelings as he always did.

Now, in the light of a new day, he wanted to hear her voice. He needed to make sure she was all right after her meeting last night, but he hesitated. The thing he'd cautioned himself about was happening—he was becoming too interested in Rachel.

He needed to slow down. He still knew very little about Rachel. She didn't give the impression of a woman whose head could be swayed by wealth, but she had made that statement the night before that had sent warnings flashing in his mind.

A job that pays me a lot is important to me, she'd said.

Perhaps she was like other women he'd dated, only interested in money. If that was the case, the sooner he found out the better off he'd be. His lips thinned into a straight line and he reached for the cell phone.

She answered on the first ring. "Good morning, Matt."

His breath caught in his throat at the sultry tone of her voice. "How did you know it was me?"

Rachel laughed and he thought of how her eyes crinkled

at the corners. He wished he could see what she looked like at that moment. "I'm not psychic. Caller ID told me."

He chuckled. "Of course. I just called to see how you're doing this morning."

"I'm fine. In fact, I was just thinking about how you scared me when you grabbed my arm last night. I thought the source had followed me back to my car."

"You should have seen your face. But I really didn't mean to scare you. I was afraid something had happened."

"Well, I'm fine this morning. I've been thinking about what he told me and I'm looking forward to tonight."

Matt let out a long breath. "Don't get your hopes up, Rachel. As far as we know, this meeting between the Rangers and the Vipers may not tell us anything. It may be the beginning of a truce between the groups."

"If my source is right and there is a vigilante, maybe they can come to some kind of understanding. I'd sure like to see the crime rate go down."

"That's what I've been hoping ever since I became a policeman."

"Then maybe we'll see something positive happen at Pepper's Bar tonight."

"Maybe so. I'll pick you up at your apartment about ten o'clock. That should give us time to get in position. I'll be in my undercover car at the front entrance."

"I'll see you then. Bye."

The call disconnected and Matt stared at the phone in his hand. Why hadn't he asked her to dinner again? He started to punch in her number again, but then he shook his head. Slipping the phone in his pocket, he climbed from the car. He was taking her to dinner and the ballet tomorrow night. He needed to remember he was a policeman going to a stakeout like he'd done so many times in the past. The only difference was that this time the woman accompanying him could prove to be a distraction. He had to make sure that didn't happen.

* * *

His cell phone, still hooked to the charger, lay on the dresser where he'd placed it the night before. He picked it up and smiled. The icon on his BlackBerry alerted him that Rachel Long had some phone messages he hadn't heard.

He carried the phone into the kitchen, poured himself another cup of coffee and sat down at the kitchen table. So far the messages he'd retrieved from her cell phone had been to David Foreman, the man she called her second father, one to her mother and one to Matt Franklin about picking him up for dinner. Nothing of much interest. Although he did wonder what was up between Matt and Rachel.

His eyes grew wide as he heard Rachel and Matt discussing a meeting she'd had with a source last night and how Matt had scared her when she returned to the car. He sat up straight when they mentioned the meeting at Pepper's Bar tonight.

Rage filled him and he pounded his fist on the table. They knew! And he'd gone to such lengths to get the fake message to the Vipers that the Rangers wanted to meet with them.

He took a deep breath and willed himself to think. If Rachel's source had told her about the meeting, then he must be a Viper. According to Rachel's conversation, the Vipers had no clue that the Rangers wouldn't be there.

The anger he'd felt a moment ago dissolved and he began to laugh. So the *Beacon*'s star reporter and Lake City P.D.'s golden boy detective were going to be watching what happened at Pepper's Bar tonight. He'd try to give them a show they wouldn't forget.

SEVEN

Rachel and Matt scrunched into the dark recesses of a deserted apartment building's doorway. A sign across the entrance stated that the building had been condemned and wasn't suitable for habitation. Boards covered the windows on either side of the door, just as Rachel had seen on many of the buildings a few nights earlier when she'd watched two murders take place. What would she see tonight?

Across the street, a light from inside Pepper's Bar lit the sidewalk in front and revealed a small room with tables and chairs scattered about. A string of multicolored Christmas lights, the only attempt at a holiday decoration evident in the neighborhood, cast a garish glow around the two sides and top of the entrance.

Rachel strained to see if anyone was in the bar but she could see no customers. A man she assumed to be the owner sat on a stool at the bar with his attention directed to a television on the wall. This was either a slow night for business or the regulars had been warned to stay away.

At the far end of the street, lights burned in the windows of two apartment buildings that looked like they'd fallen on hard times. The people who lived there were probably much like the mother Rachel had interviewed at the last gang murder—locked inside with the shades drawn until morning.

Rachel's legs ached from standing in one spot and she

shifted her weight. Matt leaned over and whispered, "Are you all right?"

She nodded. "What time is it?"

"Nearly eleven. We should see something soon."

As if on command, a car pulled to the curb in front of the bar. Rachel held her breath and pushed back into the darkness. Matt's arm circled her shoulder. "Shhh," he whispered. "We don't want them to see us."

The pounding in her ears echoed through her body. She pressed her hand against her heart in an effort to slow the beating but it was useless. The memory of two lifeless bodies on the sidewalk flashed through her mind.

The car door on the driver's side opened and a tall man climbed out. His gaze swept the street as he buttoned his leather jacket. The back door opened and a second muscular man stepped to the curb. The two, who appeared to be in their late twenties, spoke a few words before they turned and walked into the bar.

A tingling raced up Rachel's spine and she trembled. Matt's arm tightened around her shoulders. She glanced at him out of the corner of her eye. His forehead furrowed as he studied the scene across the street. In the dim light, she could see the outline of his jaw and the muscle that twitched in the side of his face. Was he feeling fear like her, or excitement at what they were witnessing?

"Do you know either of them?" Rachel whispered.

"The second one is Big T, the head of the Vipers."

Rachel leaned closer. "They weren't what I expected. I thought most of them were teenagers."

Matt shook his head. "The gangs are getting older. Some members are well into their thirties."

Before Rachel could respond, a door slammed. A man exited the bar. It had to be the owner leaving, just like her source said. Pulling his jacket on, he hunched his shoulders against the cold and strode down the street without a backward glance. Maybe he'd seen the gangs in action too many times to argue with them about taking over his business for a short time.

Silently, Matt and Rachel watched. Inside the bar, the two Vipers sat at a table near the window. From time to time, the first man they'd seen exit the car would walk to the door and peer outside.

After fifteen minutes, Matt leaned down and whispered, "Something must have gone wrong. You stay here. I'm going to get a closer look."

Rachel clutched at his sleeve. "No, Matt. You need to stay hidden."

He pulled away. "Don't worry. I'm just going to get the license plate number of the car. If I hear anybody coming, I'll duck into one of those buildings."

Before she could voice another objection, Matt slipped from their hiding place. He flattened himself against the side of the building and eased down the street until he stood on the sidewalk directly across from the car.

Bending over, he ran across the pavement and ducked behind the car. Rachel couldn't tell if he was writing down the number. Maybe he was committing it to memory.

She cast a nervous glance up the street. He had to get away from there. The Rangers might arrive any minute and demand to know why he was snooping around.

"Come on, come on," she whispered.

The door to the bar opened and the driver stepped out. Rachel clamped her hand over her mouth to keep from screaming as he walked to the car. Matt, who still crouched by the back bumper, didn't move. The man opened the car door and pulled out a bag. Glancing around once more, he returned to the bar.

A ragged breath escaped her lips as Matt pushed into a slumped position and began to ease into the street. His eyes trained on the bar, he slowly retreated. Without warning, he stopped and flattened himself against the pavement. Rachel strained to see what was happening.

A man turned the corner and headed down the street in front of the bar. Rachel's pulse raced. Was this one of the Rangers coming to join the meeting?

The man walked slowly, as if he was out for an evening stroll. He glanced at the bar but didn't enter. The light from inside illuminated a lunch box swinging from his hand. Rachel relaxed. He must be a worker returning home after getting off second shift.

Matt evidently had decided the same. He pushed up in the crouching position again and turned toward where Rachel waited. He'd only taken two steps when the stillness of the night exploded with a deafening roar.

Propelled by the giant fireball engulfing the bar, lethal shards of glass flew in all directions. Rachel dropped to her knees and covered her face as jagged slivers rained down.

When the sound of flying debris stopped, she opened her eyes and pushed to her feet. Fire leaped through the shattered windows and the door of the bar toward the sidewalk. The men inside couldn't have survived the impact and the flames. The car, now blackened from the blast, resembled a salvage yard rusty shell.

"Matt! Matt! Where are you?"

No answer.

She rushed from her hiding place toward the last spot where she'd seen him. Glass crunched under her shoes. She jerked to a stop and shook her head in denial.

"No," she moaned.

Matt lay motionless in the street, the lunch box she'd seen in the man's hand beside him.

Rachel rushed toward Matt and dropped to her knees. He lay on his stomach, his legs spread-eagled and the right side of his face on the pavement. Above his left eye, blood gushed from a cut.

Pulling her cell phone from her purse, she punched the buttons.

"911. What's your emergency?"

"There's been an explosion at Pepper's Bar on Locust Street. There are people inside and there's an injured man in the street." Her gaze locked on the lunch box next to Matt and she swallowed back the nausea rising in her throat. "I think another man who was walking by the bar when it exploded may be hurt, too."

"Responders are on the way. Are you near the injured person?"

"Yes." She knew she screamed the word but she couldn't control her voice.

"Can you describe his injuries?"

"He's unconscious. There's a cut on his head. And there's lots of…" She choked on the word.

"What?"

She swallowed. "Blood."

"Is he breathing?"

Rachel leaned closer and placed her hand on his neck. "I can feel a pulse."

"Good. Stay with him until help gets there. Are you hurt?"

Rachel touched her face but there were no cuts. She examined her arms and legs but saw nothing out of the ordinary. "No, I'm okay. I wasn't close to the explosion."

"Then just stay calm. I'll stay on the line with you until someone arrives."

In the distance sirens wailed. "I hear them. They should be here any minute."

Flashing lights appeared down the street. Within moments fire engines, police cars and ambulances converged on the area. Rachel stood and waved at two paramedics as they jumped from their vehicle.

"Over here!"

She backed away as the men knelt over Matt.

"Are you still there?"

The voice reminded her she still held the phone to her ear. "They're here. Thank you for your help."

"They'll take care of you. I hope everything turns out all right for the victims."

Rachel closed the phone and stared down at the men giving aid to Matt. He still hadn't moved.

She pulled her attention to the firemen who were already training high-powered streams of water on the raging blaze. Giant flames licked at the roof and the surrounding buildings and cast a kaleidoscope of bright colors on the deserted storefronts.

The voice of one of the paramedics caught her attention. He leaned over Matt and spoke into his ear. "Can you hear me?"

With a groan, Matt moved his arms. "Wh-what happened?"

"You've been hurt. You need to lie still while we check you out."

Matt flattened his hands against the pavement and tried to push up. "I'm okay."

"Let's be sure before you move." The two men gently restrained him.

Matt closed his eyes, then they flew open. "Rachel? Where's Rachel?"

She stepped closer. "I'm here, Matt. I'm not hurt. Now be still and let these men do their job."

He gave a weak nod. "Glad you're okay."

Two other paramedics rushed up with a gurney. The one who still knelt by Matt glanced up at Rachel. "We're going to put him in the ambulance and check him out."

She followed as the men rolled Matt toward the vehicle, pushed the gurney into the back and climbed in after it.

"Get back! The roof's going!"

Rachel jumped at the warning yelled by one of the firefighters. The building looked like a folding house of cards as it slowly crumbled in a burning heap. She thought of the two men who'd arrived and sat near the front window waiting for a meeting and the man who'd walked by with his lunch box. Had they all died unaware they were counting down the minutes until their deaths?

From inside the ambulance, Matt moaned again. At least he was alive. The men she'd seen earlier weren't.

She stepped around the side of the vehicle and slumped against it. Her head pounded from the aftereffects of the explosion and the events of the night blinked in her mind like they were posted on a theater marquee.

The question she'd asked her source had troubled her from the beginning, and now it did more than ever. If the Rangers wanted a meeting, why would they come into the Vipers' neighborhood? Had this been the Rangers way of getting revenge on the Vipers? Or could it be something else—the work of a vigilante hoping to make it appear like Ranger retribution?

A fireman walked over to the ambulance and stopped at the open back door. Soot covered his jacket and he pulled his helmet off. "How is he?" the fireman asked.

"Just some cuts. He'll be awfully sore in the morning, but he's okay." Rachel recognized the voice of the first paramedic who'd examined Matt.

"Good. Wish I could say the same for whoever was inside the bar and the guy on the sidewalk."

The emergency responder inside the ambulance hopped to the ground. Rachel inched further away so they wouldn't see her. "Have you recovered any bodies yet?"

"Just the man outside. From the looks of things, he was in the wrong place at the wrong time," the fireman said. "We can't get to the bodies inside, though. Fire's too hot. It'll have to cool off before we can go in. Then it may not matter. Don't imagine there's much left."

"What happened? A gas leak?"

"Nope. I guess this'll be one for the arson squad and the police department. Looks like somebody tossed a Molotov cocktail through the back door."

The paramedic let out a low whistle. "You don't say. Think it was gang related?"

"Probably. That's the only kind of violence they have in this neighborhood. If we do find bodies inside, it may be good for everybody. The thugs around here don't deserve to live, but I sure hate to see another innocent victim again."

"You got that right. I'm sick and tired of answering calls to shootings in this area. No telling how many other folks around here have been caught in the cross fire lately. Most of the time we get to the scene before the police do, but we're under orders not to go in until officers arrive to cover us." He hesitated. "It's hard not to charge right in when you know children are in danger, but you can't because the shooters may still be around."

The fireman sighed. "I know. Fire department's the same way. Maybe these guys will just hurry up and kill each other off."

"We should be so lucky." The two men's voices drifted away as they ambled in the direction of the fire.

Rachel shuddered at the words she'd heard. Their statements about the gangs being responsible for the crime in the area were true. Many people probably felt the same way. But there was another side that troubled her. No matter how society would judge a person, Rachel couldn't bring herself to believe that murdering anyone was right.

She stepped to the back of the ambulance and peered inside. Matt sat on the side of the gurney. A bandage covered the left side of his forehead from his hairline to his eyebrow. Two paramedics sat across from him. He glanced at her as she stopped. "Are you ready to go?"

Her eyes widened. "Aren't you going to the hospital?"

He shook his head. "These guys tell me I'm going to be mighty sore tomorrow but I don't have life-threatening injuries. So I think we need to go."

One of the paramedics glanced at her. "We'd really like to take him to the hospital to be checked out but we can't force him."

"Doesn't he need some stitches?"

The paramedic shook his head. "The cut looked like it was deep because of the blood. That's typical of wounds around the head. It'll heal all right without stitches."

Matt eased off the gurney and climbed from the ambulance. When he reached the ground, he swayed toward Rachel and grabbed hold of the side of the ambulance. Steadying himself, he smiled, but Rachel spotted the tremor of his lips. "I'm fine. Let's go."

Rachel tilted her head and frowned. "Matt, I really think—"

He grabbed her arm. "We need to go now."

Before she could resist, Matt propelled her down the street in the direction of his car. Rachel stumbled trying to keep pace with his long strides. She was afraid he'd fall if she pulled away from his grasp.

"Slow down. For a guy who's just been hurt, you shouldn't be moving so fast."

The car he'd driven sat at the end of the block and he clicked the automatic door locks as they drew closer. Rachel had barely closed the door when Matt gunned the accelerator. They sped down the street.

Rachel clutched the seat belt across her body. "What's the hurry?"

Matt glanced in the rearview mirror and slowed the car. "I saw two detectives from my department arriving at the scene.

I didn't want them questioning me about what I was doing there."

"Was one of them Philip?"

"No. Neither one of us are on duty this weekend. When he left the office this afternoon, he said he wasn't feeling well. He thought he had a fever and was planning on going to bed as soon as he got home. No need to disturb him. Those other guys can handle this." He glanced at her. "But Monday morning I'm going to have to tell Philip and my captain about being there. I think it's time we took the theory of a vigilante more seriously."

Rachel nodded. "Did you hear those firemen talking about a Molotov cocktail?"

"Yes. I don't think those guys talking knew we were listening. It won't take the arson guys long to determine if that was the cause of the explosion. It sure looks like it to me."

Another thought struck her. "Did you hear what they said about the gang members deserving to die?"

Matt's lips pulled together in a grim line. "I did."

"And what do you think about what they said?" Rachel held her breath for Matt's answer. She had often wondered how police officers could face the violence they did every day and not become hardened in their feelings toward lawbreakers.

Matt sighed and reached up to touch the bandage on his face. "I understand their frustration, but as a Christian, I have to think of it in a different way. I'm sorry for the victims of the crimes. On the other hand, I can't condone killing someone, no matter who it is."

Rachel smiled. That was the answer she'd wanted. "I'm glad to hear you say that, Matt."

Fifteen minutes later Matt stopped at her apartment building entrance. Rachel turned to him. "Would you like to come in for a cup of coffee? It's the least I can do for you after almost getting you killed tonight."

Matt chuckled and shook his head. "I think I'd better get

on home. Besides, I'm sure you have a story to write and I wouldn't want to distract you from that."

She smiled. "You're right about the story. I'll send it in before I go so bed so that it can make the morning edition." She leaned forward and studied the bandage on his forehead. "Are you sure you're going to be all right?"

He nodded. "Yes, I'll be fine by tomorrow night. Don't forget. We have a date for dinner and the ballet."

Her heart raced at the way he stared into her eyes. "I'm looking forward to it. I've never been to a ballet before."

"So I'll see you then."

She reached for the handle to open the door but stopped. Turning back to Matt, she took a deep breath and let her gaze travel over the bandage on his forehead. "I'm sorry you were hurt tonight, but I'm glad you were there with me. Thank you for being such a good friend."

His Adam's apple bobbed as he swallowed. "I'm glad we're friends, Rachel."

"Me, too." She opened the door and hopped out.

As the car pulled out of the parking lot, the memory of Matt lying in the street returned and she shuddered. She'd never felt such a sense of terror and helplessness at the same time. She remembered screaming his name as she hurried to him. The thought of the sight of his blood on the pavement still sent goose bumps up her spine.

Since becoming a reporter, she'd witnessed violent crime scenes and accidents that left people injured, but she'd never reacted as she did tonight. The difference was that the person who'd been hurt was Matt, and it had terrified her to see him injured and bleeding. She'd told him she was glad they were friends, but she couldn't let it go any further.

All she had to do was concentrate on other things like her job, and now was a good time to start. She had a story to write and a career to build. There was no time for anything else. Maybe if she told herself that often enough, she might even come to believe it.

EIGHT

He reached outside his apartment door and picked up the morning newspaper. Carrying it back to the kitchen table, he sat down, picked up his cup of coffee and opened to the front page. He took a sip from his cup and spewed the hot coffee from his mouth at the sight of the *Beacon*'s headline. Three Die in Fiery Explosion at Bar.

"Three?" he screamed, then clamped his mouth shut for fear the neighbors would hear.

He scanned the story quickly, his heart beating faster with each word. When he finished, he hurled the newspaper to the table, stood and began to pace back and forth across the kitchen.

When he threw that Molotov cocktail into the rear of the building, he knew the two Vipers were there. The innocent man on the sidewalk was a complete surprise. He rubbed his hands over his eyes as he tried to digest what he'd just read.

This couldn't be happening. His goal when he'd started his campaign was to alternate his victims between the two gangs. That way they would soon think their rival was the murderer and declare all-out war with each other. Then the police could step in and arrest the remaining members.

The streets of Lake City would at last be free of the hoodlums who ruled their neighborhoods with fear and violence. With the end of the gangs, he could live in the knowledge that his secret campaign had brought about good. Children could play safely outside their homes and residents could walk without fear on the streets.

He clenched his fist and banged the kitchen cabinet. Now in his quest he had killed an innocent person—a man returning home from work. He closed his eyes, spread his fingers on either side of his head and groaned. He'd never wanted that. How did this happen?

His eyes popped open and he lowered his hands. His mouth clenched into a straight line and he gritted his teeth. It was that reporter's fault. Because of her stories, he'd decided to make a bigger effort in his executions. His initial plan had been to shoot the Vipers down as they got out of their car at the bar but he'd changed his mind after reading Rachel Long's story about the possibility of a vigilante in Lake City. Pictures of a burning building would look better on the front page. So he'd decided on the firebomb.

Yes, it was her fault he'd made a mistake. With the gang members' deaths, he'd found pride. Now he knew he had become no better than they were. He had killed an innocent man. Instead of a hero, he was now a murderer.

Hatred boiled over in his heart. He grabbed the newspaper from the table and stuffed it in the wastebasket. That reporter would pay for what she'd done. Thanks to her, he was now a murderer. One more victim would make no difference.

Over the past few years Rachel had come to look forward to the Saturday mornings she and her friend Mindy spent catching up on what had happened during the workweek. This morning she had a lot to tell Mindy.

Rachel drove through the back entrance of the parking lot at The Coffee Bean and pulled into the only unoccupied space left by the usual 10:00 a.m. Saturday crowd. Climbing from the car, she hurried toward the front of the building. As she rounded the corner, she froze in place. "Not again."

The small gasp sounded like a whisper as it left her mouth. A few feet away, next to the entrance to the coffee shop, a Santa, standing beside a kettle, rang a bell for donations. He caught sight of her and gave his bell an extra shake in her direction.

"Ho, ho, ho! Merry Christmas!" The Santa's beard and mustache jiggled as his voice rose above the traffic noise.

The black belt pulled around the waist of the red suit appeared to strain at his girth. This wasn't the man who'd stolen her purse. Her rogue Santa had been thinner.

Rachel pulled out some money, inched closer and dropped it in the kettle. "There you go."

With a twinkle in his eye, he winked. "God bless you, and a merry Christmas."

Rachel took a step backward and collided with someone behind her. "So you believe in Santa again?".

Startled, Rachel turned and stared into Matt's face. The bandage on his forehead sent the events of the night before rushing through her. She blotted the picture of Matt lying in the street from her mind and tried to smile. "You scared me. Why aren't you home taking it easy this morning?"

He pointed to the paper tucked under his arm. "I thought I'd grab a cup of coffee while I read your story."

Rachel inclined her head toward the coffee shop. "I'm meeting Mindy and brought mine in case she hadn't read it."

Matt nodded. "I know Mindy. She's in our Bible study class at church."

"I know," Rachel murmured. "She's been trying to get me to come."

Matt tilted his head to one side and smiled. "I believe I invited you, too."

"And I'm going to come."

"Good."

She glanced at the Santa who was now occupied with

another donor and heaved a sigh of relief. "You really did scare me."

"Sorry. I started inside and couldn't resist seeing if you'd overcome your fear of Santa Claus."

She swatted at his arm and frowned. "With all we've been through in the last few days, I think it's understandable I'd be careful."

"You're right to be careful, Rachel. I hope you'll remember that." The laughter in his eyes had been replaced by a serious look. The words and their concerned tone set her heart to racing.

He grasped the handle of the door and held it open for her to walk inside. She glanced around for Mindy and spotted her at a table in the back. She tossed a wave in Mindy's direction and stepped to the end of the line of people waiting to place their orders. Matt stopped behind her.

Laughter and the hum of voices sent a surge of happiness flowing through Rachel. The room radiated a holiday spirit. Bright shopping bags that bulged with wrapped presents sat on the floor at the customers' feet. The white lights on the branches of a tall artificial tree blinked in the corner of the room, reminding everyone that Christmas, the most wonderful time of year, would soon be here.

She pointed to the tree and the packages underneath. "Isn't that tree beautiful?"

Matt nodded. "Yeah. I love this time of year."

"So do I. I'm sure my sister is getting more excited every day. She loves Christmas morning."

"Are you spending Christmas with your family?" Matt asked.

Rachel's eyebrows lifted. "Of course. Where else would I be?"

Matt shrugged. "I don't know. Some families don't get together. I just wondered about yours."

His eyes clouded, and Rachel frowned. "And what about you? Won't you be with your family?"

He shook his head. "I doubt it. My mother is out of the country and my father is too busy with his new wife to wonder where I'll spend the holidays."

Rachel's heart pricked at his words. For a moment she wished she could put her arms around him and make the hurt she saw in his face disappear. She struggled to find the right thing to say but the person in front of her picked up his order and stepped out of the line.

The young woman at the cash register smiled. "May I help you?"

An assortment of muffins and cookies lined trays inside the case next to the cash register. Rachel could almost hear the calorie-filled goodies calling her name and her stomach growled in anticipation.

"A bear claw or a cream cheese Danish?" Rachel bit her lip and debated the choices. Out of the corner of her eye she could see a big grin on Matt's face. She gave into her craving. "Oh, give me a bear claw, a cream cheese Danish and a cup of hazelnut coffee."

He leaned closer and whispered, "What army are you feeding today?"

Rachel glanced at the bandage on his head and her holiday spirit dampened. "I'm celebrating the fact that we're both alive this morning." Her chin quivered. "I was so scared last night when I saw you unconscious."

His eyes softened. "I'm glad to know you cared whether or not I was hurt."

"Here's your coffee." The voice of the woman behind the counter kept her from replying. Opening her purse, she pulled some bills from her wallet and handed them across the counter. As she picked up the tray holding her coffee and pastries, her hands trembled. Matt leaned around her and brushed against her arm.

"Just coffee for me."

As they stepped away from the counter, their purchases clutched in their hands, Rachel pointed to Mindy. "Want to join us?"

Matt hesitated before he responded. "I'd better not. I told the pastor I'd meet him at the church this morning to help with some projects. I should be through by lunch. Don't forget about our date tonight. I'll pick you up about seven. If it's okay with you, we can have a late supper after the ballet."

Rachel smiled. "That sounds great. Have a good day."

He smiled. "I will."

Rachel watched him go before she turned toward the table where Mindy sat, her arms crossed. Rachel eased into the chair across from her and set her pastries and coffee down.

"What?"

"You and Matt seemed awfully friendly."

Rachel sighed. "Matt's a friend. You know I can't get involved with a man."

Mindy propped her elbows on the table and held her coffee with both hands. Gazing over the top of the cup, she stared at Rachel. "How many times do I have to tell you that you can't let Cara's condition dictate how you live your life?"

Rachel shook her head. "We've been friends since high school, Mindy. You of all people should know how I feel."

"I do, but I don't think you're being realistic about your situation."

Rachel wrapped her fingers around her cup and frowned. Leaning forward, she stared into Mindy's eyes. "My father left us because he couldn't deal with Cara's disabilities, and I'm determined I won't be like him. When my mother's gone, I'll be the only family that Cara has left. You can't imagine what care for her can cost. In addition to medical costs there's adult day care and all kinds of therapy—physical, occupational and speech. And who knows what the future holds? The money

I've saved so far won't be enough for the things she may need later on."

Mindy nodded. "I admire your devotion to your sister. But you can't give up on your own life. Just because Justin demanded that you had to choose either your family or him doesn't mean every other man is going to do the same. In your heart I know you want marriage and a family."

Rachel shook her head. "I've loved two men, my father and Justin, and both of them walked out on me because of Cara. I won't go through that again. All I can think about is how I'm going to advance my career to make enough money to support Cara as she gets older." Rachel took a sip of coffee and welcomed the burning heat. "No, I'll have to leave love and marriage to others. I don't need them."

Even as she voiced the words, her heart cried out that she was wrong. She did need love. In fact, she longed for it, but she had convinced herself years ago what she wanted didn't matter. Cara was the important one. She had no one to take care of her but Rachel and their mother, and she'd promised her sister she'd always be there for her. If that meant ignoring feelings for Matt Franklin, she could do it. She might not want to but she had to make sure she didn't become more involved with the man who affected her as none other ever had.

Hours later Rachel stood in front of the full-length mirror in her bedroom and examined her reflection. The dress she wore had been given to her by her mother to wear to a dinner party her editor had given before Thanksgiving. At the time Rachel had felt self-conscious in the red chiffon with the flowing paneled skirt that fell from a sequined, fitted waist, but Mindy had assured her she looked great.

Rachel ran her hands down the skirt and wondered if she should change. When she'd worn it before, the cross necklace had looked perfect with the squared neck and filmy sleeves. Now with the necklace gone, the neckline looked empty. She worried that the whole dress looked wrong, especially because of the way the sequins sparkled and the fabric swayed with her every move. Maybe she needed to wear something more conservative. After all, she wasn't trying to impress Matt.

She reached for the zipper in the back just as her cell phone rang. The caller ID flashed Mindy's name.

"Hello, Mindy." She accented the name with a long sigh.

A giggle sounded on the phone. "Don't get dramatic with me. I know you. And right about now you're beginning to question whether or not you need to change clothes. Am I right?"

Rachel couldn't help but laugh. "You know me too well. I was just about to take off my dress and put on something a little more conservative."

"That's what I was afraid of. What are you wearing?"

"The red chiffon my mother gave me."

"Meeeeeooow!" Mindy purred. "Perfect choice. The way you look in that dress ought to impress Matt."

"I've told you I'm not out to impress Matt."

"Well, whatever, the red dress is perfect for the ballet and dinner. Don't you dare change. I know you look gorgeous."

"Mindy, I really think—" The ringing of the doorbell interrupted her. Rachel's hand froze on the phone. "Oh, Mindy, he's here. I don't have time to put on anything else."

Mindy chuckled. "Have a good time, Rachel. And tell me all about it tomorrow."

"I will."

Rachel disconnected the call and glanced in the mirror once more. Rubbing her lips together, she checked her lipstick, picked up her jacket and headed to the door. When she opened it, Matt stood in the hall. His eyebrows shot up and his gaze traveled over her.

His smile made her heart leap. "Wow! You look gorgeous."

Rachel's face warmed and she ducked her head. "Thank you, kind sir."

He reached for her coat and held it while she slipped it on. As he pushed it on her shoulders, he leaned closer and she could feel his warm breath on her neck. "I'm glad you're going with me tonight, Rachel."

She turned and stared into his eyes. "Thank you for inviting me."

He cleared his throat and crooked his arm. "Then let's go."

She slipped her arm in his and they walked down the hallway to the elevator. As they waited, she turned to Matt. "This elevator can be slow at times. I've talked to the owner about moving to a first-floor apartment, but for the time being I'm stuck up here on three. What about you? Do you have an apartment or a house?"

Matt turned his head away from her. "I live in a condo."

Rachel's eyes widened. "A condo? There aren't many of those in Lake City. Which one do you live in?"

"Emerald Basin."

"Emerald Basin?" she said. "That's a double-gated condominium community out toward the lake."

He reached over and punched the elevator button again. "I know."

Matt didn't turn toward her and his profile appeared impassive. Emerald Basin? She couldn't believe it. Only the wealthy lived there, not usually people who worked for the police department. She wouldn't have been more surprised if he had told her he lived in a homeless shelter.

She swallowed and tried to regain her voice. "Matt, why have you never told me you live in the most expensive area of the city?"

He turned to her. The icy stare he directed at her chilled her. "I never thought it was important."

The elevator arrived and they stepped inside. Neither spoke

all the way to the ground level or after they exited the building. Matt took her arm and steered her across the street to his car. She halted, surprised again, at the sleek, black sports car in front of them.

"I-is this your car?"

He bit his lip. "Yes."

She glanced up at him. "But I've never seen you drive this before."

"Every time you've seen me I've been in one of the department's cars."

He unlocked the door and held it open for her to climb inside. She snuggled into the leather seat as he slammed the door and stared in disbelief at the expensive sound system. The dials and knobs on the dash far outnumbered anything she'd ever seen. How did he ever remember what each one was for?

As Matt scooted behind the wheel, she pulled her seat belt across her lap. "Nice car."

"Thanks. It was a birthday present. The condo was, too."

She caressed the smooth leather-padded dash. "Those are some kind of presents."

"Yeah, my mother likes to make a statement."

Rachel froze at the callous sound of his voice. "Does your mother live near here?"

He cranked the motor. "No. I grew up in New York, on Long Island. She travels a lot. Haven't seen her in over a year."

"You must miss her."

The muscle in his jaw constricted. "Yeah."

The sudden chill Matt emitted puzzled Rachel. She started to ask him something more about his mother, but one glance at his rigid facial muscles changed her mind. At a loss as to what had just happened, she glanced out the window at the side view mirror. The taillights of a car parked in a spot on the opposite side of the lot flashed as the driver prepared to back out. A security light nearby illuminated the vehicle. Rachel squinted to get a better view. Something looked familiar.

Her eyes grew wide and her breath caught in her throat. The sight of a dent in the back fender and chipped paint across the trunk sent goose bumps racing down Rachel's spine. It was the car the young man had driven away after following her from the *Beacon*'s lobby.

Matt backed his car out and headed toward the parking lot entrance. Her puzzlement at Matt's sudden silence vanished as the car pulled from its spot and followed them onto the main street.

The car trailed behind with no attempt to pass on the four-lane street. She gripped the sides of her seat and swiveled to glance behind. The car maintained its steady distance.

A few hundred feet down the road, a red light marked a major intersection. Maybe if the car pulled up beside of them in the adjacent lane she could tell if the driver was the same person she'd spotted at the *Beacon*.

Before they reached the junction of the two streets, the light turned green and Matt drove on. Rachel twisted in her seat and glanced behind again. The car turned right and accelerated down the street. She caught a glimpse of the taillights disappearing in the distance and breathed a sigh of relief.

Matt cast a sideways glance at her. "What's wrong?"

Maybe she should tell Matt about the strange young man and the car with the dented fender. One glance at his face told her this wasn't the time. She could tell him later.

"Nothing."

Had she been imagining it or was the young man in the dented car really following her? He could be a gang member. Perhaps a Ranger who wanted to put an end to her stories. Or he could be the sniper. And if he was, did he have a connection to the Santa who stole her purse?

She frowned and shook her head. The answers to those questions would have to wait until later. Right now she wanted to concentrate on an evening at the ballet and dinner with Matt. From the moment she'd expressed surprise at where he lived and his car, his attitude had changed. She had no idea what she'd done, but something told her this would probably be their one and only date.

NINE

Matt couldn't believe he was sitting across the table from Rachel in his favorite Italian restaurant. The dining area looked beautiful tonight with the huge Christmas wreaths decorating the walls and the candles on the tables casting a glow about the room. The soft tones of a flute accompanied by a piano vibrated through the room as the musicians performed a medley of Christmas carols. He'd wanted to bring her here for weeks but he'd put off asking her. Now here they were. He hoped she was enjoying the evening as much as he was.

They'd gotten off to a shaky start at her apartment when he told her about his home and car. In the past when his family's wealth had been revealed, dollar signs flashed in his date's eyes and the questions began. Rachel hadn't reacted that way. He wondered why.

At the ballet, she'd appeared engrossed in the music and the dancers. When she did take her eyes off the stage, it was only to flash a happy smile in his direction. Now as he watched her, she closed her eyes, swallowed the last bite of her tiramisu and gave a moan of pleasure.

After a moment she opened her eyes. "That is a delicious dessert."

He chuckled and picked up his coffee cup. "Does it rank up there with bear claws and cream cheese Danishes?"

A scowl crossed her face and she shook a finger at him.

"Don't remind me of how many calories I've eaten today. It's depressing to think of how many hours I'll have to spend in the gym this week."

He laughed and set his cup down. "How did you enjoy the ballet?"

Her face grew serious and she stared into his eyes. "It was wonderful. Thank you so much for taking me. I've never been to a ballet before."

His eyebrow arched. "Really? Never?"

She shook her head. "In my family we never had money for extra things like the ballet or the theater. Sometimes I'd hear girls at school talking about going to see *The Nutcracker* and I'd wish that someday I would be able to do that." She reached across the table and squeezed his hand. "Thank you for making my wish come true, Matt."

The touch of her hand made his skin tingle. He slipped his fingers from hers. "I'm glad I could be of help."

A hurt look flashed in her eyes for a moment before she tucked a strand of her blond hair behind her ear and sat up straighter. "I suppose things like the ballet were common in your family. From the look of your car and now knowing where you live, I'd say you must have had a very privileged childhood."

He nodded. "I suppose you could say that. My mother inherited a lot of money from her father, and she intended for her only child to have everything money could buy. She's still that way."

Rachel's eyes grew wide. "Wow. I can't imagine how wonderful that would be."

He reached for his water glass and circled the top with his finger. "It's not as good as it sounds. From the furthest time I can remember, my mother was never home. She was too busy with her social life. My father was off chasing the latest young woman who appealed to him. I had many nannies and staff to provide for me but they didn't really care about me. I was just their job."

Her forehead puckered with a frown. "I'm sorry. I understand about someone not caring. My father left us when my sister, Cara, was born. He couldn't deal with all her disabilities. We never heard from him again." Tears glistened in the corner of her eyes. "I still can't understand how he could turn his back on us and walk away like we were nothing. I could never tell you how difficult it was for my mother to provide for Cara and me."

His heart hurt at the agony in her words. "Well, your mother did a good job with you. Maybe I'll get to meet your mother and Cara someday."

Her body stiffened and she sat up straighter. "Maybe. My mother is a wonderful person, but I worry about her. She's getting older. I know that soon I'll have to take over a lot of the responsibility of Cara. In fact, someday I'll have the total care of her."

"Oh?"

She took a deep breath. "Yes, and it's expensive. My focus right now is to get a job that pays better. I need money for the future and I have to figure a way to get lots of it."

"Money's not everything, Rachel."

She tilted her head to one side. "Not if you've always had it. To those of us who struggle to meet our daily obligations, it's very important."

"I suppose so."

He laid his napkin on the table and motioned for the waitress to bring the check. There was no use prolonging this date. As much as he had hoped, there wasn't a relationship in the future for Rachel and him.

He tried to ignore the ache that cut into his heart but it was impossible. From the first time he'd met Rachel, he'd known she was special, but her honesty about wanting to get more money concerned him. He'd been hurt before by women who were only interested in his family's wealth, and he was determined not to go through that again. Much as he disliked the idea, perhaps it would be better if he and Rachel ended their friendship now before it got more complicated.

Rachel watched Matt pull a wad of bills from his wallet and stuff them in the bill folder the waitress had left. He didn't even appear to count out the money. Just stuck it inside as if he couldn't wait to get it out of his hands fast enough. What was the matter with him? Twice tonight she'd watched his emotions close down. Once in the car and now in the restaurant. And both times they'd been discussing the luxuries that money provides.

He glanced at her. "Are you ready to go?"

She nodded and reached for her coat on the back of her chair before she remembered Matt had checked it with a hostess when they entered the restaurant. "I need my coat."

"I'll get it for you if you want to wait in the lobby for me."

He turned and strode across the restaurant toward the coat check room. His rigid back and shoulders made her feel like a young child who'd been reprimanded over something she'd done, but she had no idea what it was.

She walked to the front door and stared outside. Snow had fallen since they'd come in, and the sight of the changed landscape calmed her. As if on cue, the melody of "White Christmas" drifted from the direction of the musicians. A memory of pulling Cara around their yard on a sled on Christmas morning surfaced, and she smiled.

Matt Franklin's moods weren't going to upset her. It was snowing and Christmas would soon be here.

Matt stopped beside her and glanced out the doors. "Oh, it's snowing. Why don't you wait here while I get the car?"

"Okay."

He held the coat for her to put on, but this time he didn't

lean forward as he had earlier. Rachel watched him leave and wondered if she would ever know the whole story about what had happened in Matt's past to make his mood so changeable.

The ringing of her cell phone interrupted her thoughts. She pulled it from her purse and frowned at the caller ID. Private number? No one she knew blocked their number.

"Hello?"

"Good evening, Miss Long. Did you enjoy the ballet?" The raspy voice was unfamiliar.

A tremor rippled through Rachel's body. "Who is this?"

A soft laugh echoed in her ear. "It doesn't matter who I am. But I know who you are."

The hand holding the phone shook. "What do you want?"

"Why, nothing." A hint of surprise laced the words. "I just wanted you to know I've been reading your stories. You're making quite a name for yourself in Lake City."

"I only report the news."

"Ah, the news. You've reported quite a bit lately about the gangs. Doesn't it ever scare you that they might decide you're a threat to them? They might even decide to harm you in some way."

Rachel didn't like the way this conversation was going and summoned every bit of courage she possessed. "I'm not afraid of them. Now tell me what you want or I'm going to hang up."

"That would be a mistake, Miss Long. I only wanted to tell you that I've been watching you. I especially like that red dress you're wearing tonight. I have a cross necklace that would look great with it."

The words hit Rachel like a punch in the stomach. "W-w-who are you?"

"We met outside your office. I'm sorry I had to hurry away so quickly but I had to get back to the North Pole and check my list for all the good little boys and girls. Unfortunately, your name wasn't on there."

"Look, whoever you are, this isn't funny. Are you the creep who stole my purse?" Rachel struggled to keep from screaming.

He sighed and the sound sent shivers down her back. "Don't you want to know if I also took a shot at you and if I set off some fireworks at Pepper's Bar?"

Rachel sucked in her breath. "You're the vigilante."

"Vigilante? I prefer to call myself a gallant knight who wants to rid this town of vermin. You wouldn't let me do that. So now I'm going to make you pay." Hatred oozed from the words.

Rachel could hardly breathe. "What are you going to do?"

"Remember the man with the lunch box?" His words fell like thunder on her ears. "You're going to be just as dead as he is. Watch out for me, Rachel. I'm coming for you."

The call ended but Rachel couldn't pull the phone from her ear. How did he know she was going to the ballet? And the red dress? He said he was watching her. Was he close now?

She spun around and let her frightened gaze dart about the room. Her gaze fell on a table near the back of the room. The man sitting there looked up from his plate, frowned and rose from his chair.

Smothering a cry for help, Rachel whirled and bolted through the double doors of the restaurant.

Matt pulled to a stop in front of the restaurant and waited for Rachel to exit. He leaned over the passenger seat and stared through the car window. She stood inside the front door with her back turned and her cell phone pressed to her ear.

When she didn't turn around, he shoved the gearshift into Park and climbed out of the car. He hurried across the snow-covered sidewalk and had just reached out to open the door when Rachel whirled, barreled through the doors and plowed into him.

She screamed at the contact with his body and jerked away. Grabbing her by the arms, Matt steadied her and pulled her closer. She struggled to twist out of his grasp and her head lolled backward. Stark terror radiated from her eyes.

His lips stretched taut across his teeth and he gave her a gentle shake. "Rachel, what's the matter?"

She glanced up at him as if seeing him for the first time. Then she threw her arms around him. He tightened his embrace and she clung to him like a frightened child. When she didn't answer, he prodded her again. "Rachel, tell me what happened."

She pulled away and glanced over her shoulder. "That man was after me."

He peered past her and tried to get a glimpse of someone in the restaurant. "A man in the restaurant?" Matt took her by the arm and stepped to the door. "What man?"

Rachel pointed at a man who was making his way across the dining room. "Th-that one."

The man sidestepped one table, then stopped at another where an elderly couple were seated. He bent over to say something to the woman, then walked behind her and scooted her chair closer to the table. The lady smiled up at him and patted his arm before he returned to his table.

Matt heaved a sigh of relief. "He was only helping an elderly woman. What made you think he was after you?"

Rachel stood transfixed, staring through the front door. She slowly raised the cell phone she had clutched in her hand. "A man on the phone said he was watching me. He said I was going to die just like the man with the lunch box."

"What?" Matt grasped her arms tighter.

She nodded. "He called while you were getting the car."

The engine hummed in his ear and Matt remembered he'd left the car running when he went to get Rachel. He turned her toward the vehicle and steered her down the steps. "Let me get you in the car where it's warm."

"Y-y-yes." Her teeth chattered as if she was freezing, but Matt suspected it was from fear.

Once inside the car, he swiveled in the seat. "Now tell me exactly what happened."

Rachel took a deep breath and related the phone conversation she'd had while she waited for him. Matt's heart beat faster with every word. When she'd finished, he reached across and wrapped his fingers around hers. Earlier he had pulled away from her. Then her hands had been warm. Now they were cold and stiff with fear.

He stroked her hand for several seconds before he spoke. "It seems obvious that your caller was the Santa who stole your purse and most likely the sniper as well. Maybe he's trying to scare you."

The fear in her eyes told him she didn't believe that. "You didn't hear him. He sounded like he hates me."

Matt reached across and buckled her seat belt around her. Placing a finger under her chin, he lifted her head until she stared into his eyes. At that moment, Matt knew he would do anything he could to protect Rachel. Later he would have time to sort out his feelings for her.

"Don't worry," he whispered. "I'm not going to let that killer get close to you. I promise you that."

Her chin trembled and a tear slipped from the corner of her eye. "Thank you, Matt."

His gaze locked on her lips. He wanted to seal his promise with a kiss but he couldn't be distracted from the promise he'd just made. The problem was that he had to figure out a way to keep it.

TEN

When Matt had picked Rachel up earlier for the ballet, she had met him at the door. Now he sat on the couch in her small living room and sipped a steaming cup of coffee. Her hands shook as she raised her cup. Color was beginning to return to her pale face. He winced at the memory of how frightened she'd looked when she ran from the restaurant.

He set his cup on the coffee table and glanced at her. "Are you feeling better?"

She nodded and wrapped her fingers around her cup. "Yes, thanks."

She smiled at him and his heart did flip-flops. His earlier resolve to end his relationship with Rachel melted. Being with her could get to be an addiction, and Matt had no idea how to overcome it.

He glanced around the apartment in an effort to divert his thoughts. "You've done a great job decorating this place. I had no idea you were a talented interior designer."

She chuckled and set her cup down. "I'm afraid I can't take credit for most of it. My mother helped me. We searched flea markets and secondhand stores until we came up with enough furniture to get me started." Her gaze drifted around the room. "But it's home to me, and I love it."

"Do your mother and sister live nearby?"

She nodded. "Just outside of town." She reached over to a

table at the end of the couch and picked up a picture frame. She ran her fingers over the glass before she handed it to him. "This is my family."

Matt gazed at the picture of Rachel, her mother and her younger sister. The mother looked very much like an older version of Rachel. It was the younger sister, however, that drew his attention. The rounded face and almond-shaped eyes made the signs of Down syndrome unmistakable, but the smile on the girl's face radiated joy like none he'd ever seen. Rachel sat next to her, their fingers laced together, and their mother stood behind with a protective hand on each one's shoulder.

Matt glanced up and Rachel was studying him with an intense look. "Three beautiful women. Your family is lovely."

Rachel bit her lip and reached for the tray on the table. Without a word she hurried from the room. He could hear the rattle of dishes in the kitchen.

Matt's fingers gripped the frame tighter. He closed his eyes and wondered what it would be like to come home in the evenings to a family. Growing up, he'd only known life with his staff, never a real family. There was no telling what country his mother was in tonight.

Rubbing his eyes to erase the hunger for the woman who was like a stranger to him, he rose, shoved his hands in his pockets and stepped to the balcony doors. He pulled the curtain back and stared down. A car drove into the apartment building parking lot. A young man got out and hurried around to the passenger side.

Matt watched the man open the car door and assist a woman from inside. She stepped close to him and he bent to kiss her. The couple pulled away from each other, laughed and headed into the building.

That's what he wanted. A woman who would love him and not be swayed by his family's money. Swallowing back the loneliness he'd felt for years, Matt let the curtain drift from his hand. He rubbed the back of his neck and turned as Rachel reentered the room.

The light from overhead glimmered in her blond hair and he thought she'd never been more beautiful. He cleared his throat and moved back to the couch.

"We need to talk about your phone call."

Her eyes clouded. "I know. What do you think I should do, Matt?"

"Well, I'll make a report about it. Until this guy is caught, I think you need to do everything possible to protect yourself."

"Like what?"

"You don't need to go off by yourself, especially to meet that source. He may be involved in this more than we know. And I think I need to stick close to you."

She shook her head. "I have a job and so do you. There's no way you can be with me twenty-four hours a day."

"I know, but Philip will help out. We can pick you up and take you to work."

Her eyes grew wide. "Matt, there's no need for that. I knew when I became a reporter that I might find myself in some dangerous situations. I know how to be careful." She swallowed and straightened her shoulders. "Really, you don't have to worry. After all, it's not your problem."

Matt wanted to pull her into his arms. How he wished he could whisper to her that she'd become his problem since the first time he saw her. Instead he frowned. "It's my job to see that every citizen is safe."

She nodded. "I understand that, but I can't let you and Philip ignore other duties just for me."

He realized arguing with her was going to do no good. Perhaps he should take it one day at a time. He exhaled and rubbed the back of his neck. "You are one of the most stubborn women I've ever met, but I see your point. Why don't we see how things go for the next few days and then decide what we need to do?"

"That sounds good to me."

"So, how about going to church with me tomorrow? You came with Mindy last Sunday. I'd really like for you to go with me."

She hesitated for a brief second and he thought she was going to decline. Then she smiled. "I'd love it. Do you want me to meet you there?"

"No, I'll pick you up. Say ten o'clock? Then we can have lunch somewhere afterward."

She chewed on her lip for a moment. "We could have lunch here if you'd agree to do me a favor."

"What is it?"

"I'd like to put up my Christmas tree tomorrow afternoon. Would you be willing to help?"

Matt's heart thudded in his chest. When he was a child, he'd always wished he could help decorate the tree in their home but his mother always hired the most expensive floral decorators in New York to turn their home into a showcase. He'd promised himself when he grew up, he'd have a tree like he wanted, but he hadn't decorated for Christmas since leaving home. The fact that Rachel lived alone and still followed tradition thrilled him.

"I'd be honored to help."

"Good. Then I'll dig out all the boxes tonight and have them ready for us tomorrow."

Matt tried to reply but his emotions had kicked into gear. His evening with Rachel, his conflict over her determination to get money, the anonymous caller and now a childhood wish remembered converged in his mind to produce helplessness like he'd never known. He had to get out of there. Snatching his coat from the couch where he'd dropped it, he pulled it on. "Guess I'd better be getting home. I'll see you in the morning."

She walked to the door and opened it for him. "Even with the phone call, I had a wonderful evening. Thank you for the ballet and dinner and for being such a good friend."

"You're welcome." He brushed past her, hurried to the elevator and punched the button. As he waited, he heard the patter of footsteps and turned to see her coming toward him.

"One more thing, Matt."

"What's that?"

"Thank you for what you said about my family. You know, about the three beautiful women. No one has ever told me that Cara is beautiful."

His eyes widened. "But she is. I could see the beauty of her soul shining in her face."

Tears filled her eyes. "I've always seen it, and I'm glad you did. Cara is the most beautiful person I know."

His breath caught in his throat. "Maybe you'll introduce us sometime."

She smiled. "I'd like that." She turned back to her apartment but stopped at the doorway and waved. "See you in the morning."

The elevator door slid open and he stepped inside. He couldn't forget how scared she'd looked when she ran out of the restaurant tonight, but he also remembered the glow in her eyes when she showed him the picture of her family.

He punched the lobby button and shoved his hands in his pocket. He'd pegged Rachel earlier as a gold digger like so many other women he'd known. Now he wasn't so sure. He'd just have to see what the future held. He only hoped his heart didn't get trampled in the process.

Rachel watched the elevator close behind Matt before she reentered her apartment. When she closed the door, she leaned against it and smiled. Even with the scare of the phone call at the restaurant she had to admit this had been one of the best evenings she'd ever had. Closing her eyes, she recalled the images of the ballerinas on stage as they moved to the music.

Melodies from *The Nutcracker* played in her head, and she swayed in rhythm to the music. She imagined herself a member of the troupe and began to hum the melody from "Waltz of the Flowers." Stretching onto her tiptoes, she hummed louder and twirled across the living room, her arms fluttering at her sides.

Her movements grew bigger as she waltzed down the hallway to her bedroom. Grabbing her pajamas and robe from the closet, she directed her steps back into the hall and toward the bathroom. With a flourish she pushed the closed bathroom door open and swept into the room.

Stifling a scream, she fell against the door and clung to it to keep from sinking to her knees. A twitching she couldn't control began in her legs and worked its way up to her head. Her body shook uncontrollably with a fear greater than anything she'd ever known. She couldn't look away from the mirror and the message scrawled on its surface with her red lipstick.

Merry Christmas, Rachel. Your present from me will arrive soon.
Santa

Rachel staggered backward and grabbed the door for support. Her eyes skimmed over the mirror once more before she screamed and bolted from the bathroom.

Matt's thoughts centered on the evening he'd spent with Rachel as he drove toward home. Even with his conflicting feelings, he'd enjoyed the time they'd spent at her apartment and he looked forward to taking her to church.

The Christian music station he was listening to on the radio began to play one of his favorite songs and he leaned over to turn up the volume. His fingers tapped a drumbeat on the steering wheel as he listened.

The ring tone of his cell phone blared, the sound competing with the music from the radio. He pulled it from his pocket and stared at the caller ID. Dispatch? With a sigh he hoped he wasn't being called out on a homicide tonight. With Philip sick, he didn't look forward to working a case alone.

"Hello."

"Matt, this is Jason at dispatch. We received a call I thought you might be interested in."

Matt's eyebrows lifted. "What is it?"

"It's that newspaper reporter you and Philip went to see at the *Beacon*. Rachel Long."

His body stiffened. "Rachel? What about her?"

"She just called hysterical. Said somebody's been in her apartment. We've sent two patrol cars over there, but I thought you might want to follow up with her tomorrow."

Matt glanced in front and behind him for cars but spotted none. After a U-turn in the middle of the street, he headed in the direction he'd just come. "Thanks for letting me know, Jason."

He wished he had a siren but he didn't have one in this car. Praying that he wouldn't be stopped for speeding, he accelerated and sped down the street. It seemed forever before Rachel's apartment building came into view.

His tires squealed to a stop at the front door. He was out of the car and into the building in a flash. When the elevator doors didn't open immediately after he pushed the button, he turned and ran to the stairs. Racing up the three flights, he burst through the door onto Rachel's floor and ran down the hallway to her apartment. He banged on the closed door. A uniformed police officer opened it immediately. He pushed past the man and strode inside.

Rachel was hunched on the couch, her elbows on her knees

and her hands covering her eyes. The two officers who stood in front of her turned in his direction as he entered the room. The older of the two frowned. "Detective Franklin, what are you doing here?"

Rachel jerked to attention and shot to her feet. Matt didn't know who took the first step, but suddenly she was in his arms, her body trembling and her arms wrapped around his neck. Her cheek rested on his shoulder and he wrapped her in a protective embrace.

"It's all right," he whispered. "Tell me what happened."

She pulled back a little, took him by the hand and led him to the bathroom. "After you left, I started to get ready for bed. This is what I found."

The breath left his body like he'd been kicked in the stomach when he saw the message scrawled on the bathroom mirror. He glanced at her and she started to shake again.

Taking her hand, he guided her back into the living room to the couch. He turned to the older of the two officers. Larry McDaniel had been one of the first veterans of the force he'd met when he joined the department. "Larry, is there another entrance into the apartment besides the front door?"

"Just through the balcony, and that door was locked from the inside. I don't think anybody could have climbed up the side of the building to get in that way, though."

Matt glanced back at the entrance. "And the door to the hallway hadn't been forced open." He pulled Rachel onto the couch beside him and took her hand in his. "When your purse was first stolen, we thought it was a random purse snatching. After the phone call tonight, I think we can assume it wasn't. This guy has the keys to your apartment, Rachel. Have you talked to the superintendent about getting the locks changed?"

She nodded. "I have. He told me he would do it first thing Monday morning."

Matt's brow furrowed. He chewed on his bottom lip for a

moment. "Well, you can't stay here until that's taken care of. I think you should pack a few things and go to your mother's house until then."

Rachel shivered. "You're right." She glanced up at the officers. "Do you need me to answer any more questions?"

Larry looked down at the notes he'd taken. "I think I have everything I need. We'll get the lab guys over here and dust for prints."

Matt grasped Rachel's hand, stood and pulled her to her feet. "You go pack a few things. I'll follow you to your mother's house."

Rachel's lips trembled with a weak smile. "Thanks, Matt. I appreciate it."

He watched her go down the hallway. When she entered the bedroom, he turned to the officers. "Larry, how long you guys going to be here?"

"I don't know. We'll go door to door and question the neighbors about anybody they might have seen in the building tonight." He sighed and glanced at his watch. "I doubt if they'll be glad to see us at this time of night, though."

Matt nodded. "I understand. If you don't need me, I'll go with Rachel to her mother's house and see she gets there safely. It looks like we've got a guy after her. He phoned her tonight and told her he was going to kill her."

Larry nodded. "That's what she told us." He glanced at his notes. "Then there was the car in the parking lot."

Matt's mouth gaped open. "What are you talking about?"

"The car with the dented fender and the chipped paint on the trunk."

Matt stared at the officer. "I don't know anything about that."

"I was going to tell you." Rachel emerged from the bedroom with a small suitcase in her hand. Her face was pale but she held her head high.

Matt's frown deepened as she told him about the young

man and the dented car that she had now seen twice. When she finished, he shook his head in disbelief. "Why didn't you tell me?"

Her face flushed. "I tried to convince myself it had nothing to do with the stories I was writing. Now I think I might have been wrong."

She should have told him when she spotted the car earlier. Perhaps he could have gotten a license number. One glance at her frightened face melted his anger. All he wanted was to make her feel safe.

He exhaled in hopes of putting her at ease. "It's okay, Rachel. Larry will notify dispatch to keep a lookout for a car matching that description."

Rachel walked to the officers and shook each one's hand. "Thank you for all you've done."

Larry smiled. "Glad we could help."

With a nod in the officers' direction, Matt followed her from the apartment. They didn't speak on the ride down in the elevator or when they exited the building. In the parking lot, Matt turned to her. "Do you want to drive your rental or do you want me to drive you?"

She hesitated for a moment. "I'd better drive. I'll need my car."

He wanted to tell her that she shouldn't be driving anywhere by herself but now wasn't the time for that. She was scared and all she wanted was to get to safety. That's what he wanted, too.

Matt watched her get in her car and lock the doors before he jogged to his vehicle. As they pulled out of the parking lot and drove through the late-night streets, Matt stayed close behind. His thoughts returned to the decision he'd made earlier to give up any idea he might have had about a relationship with Rachel. Now he felt more confused than ever.

His head had told him she was only interested in money but his heart kept insisting that wasn't true. He wished there was some way to know for sure. For now, he would have to concentrate on keeping her safe. There would be time for other answers after the vigilante was caught.

ELEVEN

Rachel glanced in the rearview mirror from time to time on the drive to her mother's home. When she spied the house where she grew up and turned into the driveway, her emotions calmed with the safe feeling she always had when she returned to the place that would always be home.

Even with the dark house bathed in the shadows of the night, the warmth inside those walls radiated into her soul. Peace flowed through Rachel. She could hardly wait for the protective hug of her mother.

Matt climbed from his car and stepped onto the driveway. She pointed to the house. "My mother and sister have already gone to bed. I hope my coming so late at night doesn't alarm them."

He reached in the backseat and pulled her suitcase out. "I'll walk you to the door and wait until you're inside."

They walked across the snow-covered front yard and stepped onto the porch. Rachel rang the bell and waited. After a few seconds a light came on from the direction of her mother's bedroom. Rachel waited, hoping her mother wouldn't be scared.

The front porch light flashed on, and a curtain covering the glass at the top of the front door moved. "It's just me, Mama. Rachel."

The door flew open and her mother stood there in the robe

Rachel had given her last Christmas. She clutched the robe at her neck and her frightened stare fastened on Rachel's face. "What are you doing here at this time of night?" Her gaze darted to Matt and her eyes grew even wider. "I don't think I know you."

"Mama, this is my friend Matt Franklin. He's a detective with the police department."

Her mother hesitated for a moment before she reached for Rachel and drew her inside. She pulled her into a fierce embrace, then held her at arm's length to study her. "Are you hurt?"

Rachel shook her head and motioned for Matt to come in. "No, but something has happened. My apartment was broken into tonight. Matt followed me here. We thought it might be better if I stayed with you for a few days until the superintendent can change the locks."

Her mother nodded. "Of course. You can stay here forever if you want." She turned to Matt and stuck out her hand. "Thank you, Mr. Franklin, for helping my daughter. I don't know what I'd do if something happened to her."

Matt set the suitcase down and smiled. "I understand, Mrs. Long. Rachel is quite special. She's a great newspaper reporter."

Her mother's eyes clouded and she faced Rachel. "Does this have something to do with those stories you've been writing about the gangs?"

Rachel's gaze darted to Matt. "Well, yes, but Matt needs to get home. I can explain everything after he leaves."

Her mother turned back to Matt. "I think I'd like to have a hot cup of cocoa. Can you join us, Mr. Franklin?"

He shook his head. "No, thanks. I'll give you and Rachel some time together. And please call me Matt."

"And you can call me Emily."

Rachel smiled at the look her mother directed at her. She

knew that the questions would start the minute Matt left. Had they been dating? Was he a Christian?

She took Matt by the arm and walked with him toward the door. "Thank you for everything, Matt. I guess we'll have to put off lunch and decorating my Christmas tree tomorrow. Maybe we can do it later this week."

"Oh, maybe not," her mother's voice interrupted. "Cara and I are planning to decorate our tree tomorrow afternoon. If you'd like, Matt, you can join us for lunch and then help with the tree. We'll eat after church."

Matt smiled. "I'd like that, Mrs. Long, I mean, Emily. I'll come when I get out of church."

Her mother headed toward the kitchen. "Good. We'll see you then."

They stopped at the front door and Rachel stared up at Matt. "Don't feel you have to accept my mother's invitation if you don't want to come."

His eyes widened. "I'd really like to come if you want me to."

She nodded. "Oh, I do, but you may get more female attention than you can stand. After all, we're a family of three women."

He laughed. "There's nothing wrong with being surrounded by beautiful women. I'll see you tomorrow."

Rachel watched as he hurried back to his car. Before he opened the door, he turned and waved to her. As he backed out of the driveway, she closed and locked the front door.

Was Matt just being courteous or did he really want to come to lunch? The last time she'd brought a man home with her was in college. It had only taken one afternoon of being with her family to convince him he couldn't deal with Cara.

Now she faced the situation again. Maybe it was a good thing Matt was going to be here tomorrow. She already knew Matt was becoming more important in her life each day, and she had to find out if he could accept her sister before it was too late.

She shook her head. Why was she kidding herself? It didn't make any difference how Matt felt about her family. That still didn't change the responsibility she had to provide for Cara. She needed to remember what she'd told Mindy—she had no time for love and marriage. Those things were for other people, not her.

She wiped at a tear and walked toward the kitchen. Every time she'd faced a problem in her life, her mother had insisted they could solve anything if they'd discuss it over a cup of her cocoa. This time, however, Rachel doubted if it would work.

Rachel laid her fork on her plate and groaned in satisfaction. "Mama, I don't know if you've outdone yourself with that meal or if I was hungry for home cooking."

Across the table from her Matt smiled. "I know it's the best I've had in a long time." He glanced at Cara who sat next to him and winked. "Why didn't you tell me your mom was such a great cook, Cara?"

Cara, who hadn't left Matt's side since he had arrived an hour earlier, stared up at Matt and grinned. Rachel's heart constricted with the adoration that she saw in Cara's eyes. It had been the same when she brought Justin home from college, and it had made him uncomfortable. Matt, on the other hand, appeared to be enjoying the attention. But then, he was used to working with the kids at the Youth Center. He'd probably learned how to mask his feelings long ago.

Rachel's mother stood. "Well, let's get the table cleared. I have chocolate cake for dessert."

Cara frowned and glanced toward the living room. "I want the Christmas tree."

Matt leaned back in his chair, groaned and smiled at Cara. "I'm with you. I'm so full I don't think I could eat cake right now." He leaned closer to her. "Why don't you ask your mom if we can decorate the tree and have dessert later? That way we can work off some of this good food we've had."

Cara clapped her hands and bounced up and down in her chair. She turned a beseeching look in her mother's direction. "Please, Mama."

Her mother laughed. "Very well. Let's get the dishes done. Then we can get to the tree."

Matt pushed back from the table and reached for his plate but Cara grabbed his arm. "No."

His eyes widened. "What?"

Cara pointed to her chest. "Dishes my job."

"Oh, I see." He scooted his chair up to the table and faced Rachel. "Then maybe your sister would keep me company while you do the dishes."

Cara bounded to her feet and waved her hands in the direction of the living room. "Go, Rachel. I do the dishes."

Rachel's heart warmed at the joy she saw in Cara's face. "All right. We'll get the tree inside."

Matt followed her to the front door of the house and glanced around the room as Rachel pulled a sweater from a coatrack. "Where's the tree?"

"It's in the carport. Mama bought it yesterday and left it out there until she could get it up today. I can't tell you how excited she and Cara are that we're here to help."

He pulled the door open and waited for her to step outside. "I'm glad I could come. Maybe this will make me want to put up a tree at home."

She laughed and led the way to the carport where a six-foot fir tree leaned against the wall. Matt heaved the tree to his shoulder. "Where's the stand?"

"I think it's inside."

He followed her back to the front of the house and carefully carried the tree through the front door. She pointed out the stand that her mother had set in a corner of the living room earlier that morning.

He stood the tree up straight and motioned for her to hold it. "Keep it upright until I can get the stand ready." He dropped to his knees and unscrewed the clamps for the trunk. Together they fitted the tree into the stand. Rachel held it in place as he tightened the clamps.

When he finished, he placed his hands on his hips and his gaze drifted over the tree. "That looks about right, don't you think?"

Rachel nodded, but before she could say anything, a squeal sounded behind her. Cara ran into the room and stopped beside Rachel. "Look, Rachel. It's a Christmas tree."

Rachel put her arms around her sister's shoulders and hugged her. "I know. Now we have to decorate it."

Their mother, carrying several boxes, walked in at that moment. "And here are the decorations."

While Matt and their mother draped the strings of lights around the tree, Rachel and Cara sat on the floor and pulled ornaments from the boxes. Cara's excitement grew as she laid the homemade decorations out on the floor.

Rachel surveyed the assortment of construction-paper ornaments covered in glitter. These were likely foreign to Matt, who'd probably grown up with the most expensive decorations on his tree. She glanced up and caught him studying her and Cara. Her breath caught in her throat.

"Cara and I made all of these when we were children. Mama wants only them on our tree since she says they're so special to her."

Her mother smiled. "Yes, they are." She pointed to a small cardboard square with a picture of a Christmas tree on it. "That's the first one Cara ever made. Her teacher said she looked through three magazines before she found the perfect picture for her ornament."

Rachel held up a construction-paper candy cane with glitter on it. "And I made this one in third grade."

Matt's dark eyes clouded and he turned back to the tree. "I can see why they're so important to you."

Two hours later they sat in the living room and gazed at the decorated tree. The white lights winked on and off in rhythm. Rachel studied each of the ornaments she'd loved for years and let out a contented sigh.

"That's a beautiful tree."

Her mother nodded. "More cake anyone?"

Matt set his empty plate on the coffee table and groaned. "I couldn't eat another bite. It was all delicious."

Her mother glanced at her and Rachel detected a gleam in her eye. "Then maybe you'll come again."

"I'd love to." Matt glanced at his watch. "But I'd better be getting home now. I don't want to wear out my welcome."

Cara jumped to her feet, a frown on her face. "No. Stay."

He laughed and chucked her under the chin. "I'd love to, Cara, but I have some things I need to do for work tomorrow. I'll come back soon. I promise."

Cara stuck out her bottom lip. Rachel put her arm around her. "Don't pout, Cara. Matt will come again."

He turned to her mother and shook her hand. "Thank you for the wonderful afternoon, Emily."

"We were happy to have you."

Rachel followed him to the door and grabbed her sweater. "I'll walk you to the car."

As they started out the door, Cara ran to them. She tugged on Matt's arm. "You promised."

He smiled and patted her hand. "I'll see you soon."

When they stepped outside, Rachel stuck her hands in her pockets and walked beside him to his car. "I hope you didn't feel like Cara was monopolizing you today."

His eyebrows arched. "Oh, no. I think she's wonderful."

"I think so, but I never know what someone else will think."

He glanced back toward the house. "You should have more faith in your friends."

She lifted her chin and took a deep breath. "Maybe it's the faith I placed in my friends who dropped me after meeting Cara that has colored my attitude."

"What do you mean?"

She shrugged. "When I was growing up, nobody wanted to come to my house because Cara scared them. And then my college boyfriend changed his mind about marrying me after he met Cara."

He shook his head. "Then he wasn't worthy of you, Rachel."

"I know that, but it doesn't change what my life is."

He tilted his head to one side. "And what is that?"

She struggled to hold back the tears. "From the time I was a child I've known that someday I would be totally responsible for Cara. I've seen how hard it's been for my mother. She's worked two or three jobs just to make ends meet, and she's getting older way before her time. If I'm going to take over, I have to have more money than I have now."

His lips thinned. "So money is important to you."

"Not for me. For Cara. I have no idea how I'm going to provide for her. I can't on the salary I make now. The only thing I know to do is to try for a higher paying job." She paused for a moment. "I thought about this a lot last night, and I filed a story about the vigilante this morning for tomorrow's edition. I can't let him scare me off. This may be the ticket I need to move up."

Matt stared at her for a moment. "If you're dead, you can't do Cara any good."

"Please understand, Matt. That's a chance I have to take."

He shook his head and pulled the car door open. "I can

see there's no convincing you differently. I'll pick you up for work tomorrow."

She shook her head. "I'll drive to work tomorrow. I'm not going to change my life."

He gritted his teeth and clenched his fists. "I just hope this doesn't cost you your life."

With that, he jumped into his car and roared out of the driveway. Rachel watched as he turned the corner before she headed back inside. Tears trickled from the corners of her eyes and she wiped at them.

For a few minutes this afternoon she'd felt happier than she had in years. It seemed so natural for Matt to be there with her family, but then she'd realized she was only dreaming. There was no room for a man in her life. Not even one as wonderful as Matt Franklin.

TWELVE

Rachel hummed the melody of the "Nutcracker March" as she glided down the third-floor hallway of the *Daily Beacon*. The bustle of activity in the building always excited her, but this morning it seemed more invigorating than ever. She could hardly wait to get to her office and see if her story in the morning paper had prompted any emails.

Rachel hurried into her office and sank down in the chair at her desk. She had just booted up her computer when a knock at the door caused her to turn.

"Morning, Rachel. Hope I'm not interrupting anything." Her editor, Cal Belmont, stepped into the office.

Rachel stood. "I was just getting ready to check my emails. I thought this morning's story might have attracted some responses."

Cal chuckled. "Did it ever. My email box has been flooded with messages. Seems like your story has stirred a lot of interest in our readers. That's what I like to see."

Excitement washed over her. "Really? Like what?"

He motioned to her computer. "Pull yours up and see for yourself."

Rachel sat down and opened her first email. She read it and then clicked on the next. The excitement she'd felt a moment ago burst, replaced by astonishment. Unable to believe what she was seeing, Rachel opened several more. Her chest hurt like a heavy weight sat on it. "I don't believe this. These letters support the vigilante."

A smirk pulled at Cal's mouth. "Yeah. It seems like a lot of folks think the end justifies the means. Get rid of the gang members whatever the cost. So what if a murderer is loose? He's killing the right people."

Rachel glanced at the last message she'd read. "Listen to what one guy said. 'I say hooray for an individual who's willing to stand up and take our streets back. I know a lot of guys who would be willing to help if you need us.'"

"Yeah, I was copied on that one."

"And this one," Rachel said, "'Keep up the good work, man. You're a hero to me.'" She leaned back in her chair and stared at Cal. "I can't believe anybody would write something like this."

Cal waved his hand in dismissal and laughed. "Don't worry about it, Rachel. Some people just like to blow off steam. Doesn't amount to anything."

"But, Cal, my story didn't condone murder. Many of these letters do. I wanted to let the vigilante know he's no better than the gang members." She pointed back to the computer screen. "These emails make it sound like he's some kind of hero."

"As long as we can sell newspapers, I could care less about the personal convictions of our readers. You keep the stories coming and let's try to capitalize on the emotion you've stirred up."

Rachel cocked an eyebrow. "I only reported what happened and what an apparent gang insider told me. We don't want this vigilante to become a hero."

Cal laughed. "Why should we care how people see him? We have a chance here to promote a lot of interest in our newspaper and I want to take advantage of it."

Rachel couldn't believe what she was hearing. "Cal, we need to be careful with this. We don't want to feel responsible if copycat killers take to the street. A lot of innocent people could get hurt if vigilante law becomes prevalent."

Cal's gray eyes narrowed and he pushed his wire-rimmed glasses up on his nose. "That sounds strange coming from you. I know what you're up to, Rachel. You're using your job here as a springboard to something bigger and better. You've been biding your time until the right story came along. Well, you've got one now, and I expect it to be covered the way I want it."

In the time she'd worked for Cal, Rachel had never experienced such a demanding tone in his voice. "I understand, but I haven't heard anything from my source in several days and I don't have any other leads right now. I'll let you know if things change."

Cal nodded and directed a stern glare in her direction. "Good. Just remember, if you expect a good recommendation from me when you leave here, you'd better do what I ask."

He sauntered from her office, leaving Rachel's mind whirling. Cal was right about her wanting a big story, but now that she had it she didn't know if the dangers were worth it. With her life threatened and her apartment invaded, she felt more vulnerable than she ever had. She buried her face in her hands.

A discreet cough at the door caught her attention. She tried to ignore the happiness that washed over her at the sight of Matt but it was no use. He looked so handsome this morning. She'd heard the expression "dressed to kill" many times and had never understood it. Until now. Every time she saw Matt her heart kicked into overdrive and a little more of her resolve to keep her distance from him died.

She rose and waved him into the office. "What are you doing here this morning?"

He grinned. "Checking on my favorite newspaper reporter. I wanted to see if you made it to work okay."

"Yes, Cara woke me up early and I beat the morning rush

hour." She glanced at her computer and frowned. "But I can't say I was happy at what greeted me."

"What?"

She read a few of the emails to him and related her conversation with Cal. When she'd finished, Matt rubbed the back of his neck. "Whatever happened to 'Thou shalt not kill'? Have we gotten so jaded that we think murder is okay if it serves the public need?"

Rachel nodded. "I know. But Cal wants me to play this angle up. It was almost like he wanted me to make the readers even more vocal."

Matt sighed. "Well, I suppose you have to do what your editor wants if you want to keep your job. But don't forget about the threat you had last night."

Fear knotted Rachel's stomach, but she managed a weak smile. "I won't. I'm not going to do anything foolish."

"Good, but I still think Philip and I need to keep an extra watch on you."

"That sounds good, but you have other things to take care of. I'll be fine."

His forehead wrinkled and he exhaled. After a moment he grinned. "I couldn't face Cara if anything happened to you. So call me if you see anything suspicious."

"I will. Thanks for everything, Matt." She walked around her desk and faced him. "And thank Philip for wanting to help. Is he at work or still under the weather?"

"He called in sick this morning, but I talked to him about the incident at Pepper's Bar."

"Was he angry that we didn't tell him?"

Matt shook his head. "He didn't sound like he was. He said that he liked you and would do anything to help when he came back to work."

Relief flowed through Rachel. "Good. I didn't want to be the cause of any problems between you and your partner."

"You weren't." He glanced at his watch and backed toward

the door. "I need to get back to the station. I'll call you later. Maybe we can—"

Rachel's eyes grew wide. "Matt, watch out," she yelled.

Her warning came too late. Toby Jones, the *Beacon*'s custodian, walked through the door and collided with Matt. Toby fell against the door frame and struggled to regain his balance. Whirling, Matt grabbed the elderly custodian and steadied him. "I'm sorry. I didn't see you."

Rachel rushed over and stopped beside Toby. "Are you all right?"

He nodded. "I'm fine, Miss Long. I shoulda said something instead of just barrelin' into your office. It was my fault."

Matt released Toby's arm. "That was quite a jolt. Why don't you sit down?"

Toby shook his head and backed away. "No need for that. I was passing by and thought I'd let Miss Long know I read her story. I didn't mean to cause no commotion."

Rachel smiled. "You know you can come in here any time. But about my story, what did you think?"

"I thought it was mighty good. Never thought about there being a vigilante, but it makes sense."

Rachel pointed to Matt. "This man who just ran over you is Detective Matt Franklin. With any luck he'll soon catch him." Matt nodded his agreement.

Toby looked at them as if they'd lost their minds. "Catch him? I hope you don't before he finishes what he's set out to do."

Rachel stared in disbelief. Another person who thought of the vigilante as some sort of hero? "Toby, you can't mean that."

The man's gray hair bobbed up and down as he nodded. "I sure do. The gangs are a scourge. If you don't think so, come spend one night in my neighborhood. Lock your doors at sundown, pull your shades and stay away from windows 'til morning. Then you'll understand."

"But murder—"

Toby's face mottled with red splotches. "Don't tell me 'bout murder. I see it all the time. I'm glad somebody's finally decided to do something about it. I wish I could shake the guy's hand and tell him thanks."

Rachel couldn't believe the hatred spewing from Toby's mouth. Beside her, Matt appeared to be at a loss for words also. Toby turned and walked from the office, leaving the two of them to stare after him.

"Oh, Matt," Rachel breathed. "This story has touched some deep feelings in the people of Lake City."

"Yeah. And we're both caught in the middle."

"What do we do now?"

"I don't know." He took a deep breath. "Maybe we'll get a break soon. This guy can't hide from the police forever."

Her phone rang and Rachel reached for it as Matt backed toward the door. She waved and picked up the receiver. "Hello."

"Too bad about Big T. I liked him a lot."

Rachel's eyes grew wide at the voice she knew she'd recognize anywhere. Gesturing wildly for Matt to stay, Rachel took a deep breath. "I didn't know him, but it was still horrible seeing him die that way."

Matt grabbed a notepad off her desk, scribbled something, and held it up for her to see. *Is that your source?*

Rachel nodded, and he leaned over her desk as if trying to catch part of the conversation. She put her finger to her lips for Matt to be quiet and not alert the caller that she wasn't alone.

"The brothers are really mad now. They say somebody got to pay."

Rachel slipped the pad toward her and began to make notes about what the source was saying. Matt's forehead wrinkled as he tried to read the words.

"Can't you do something to make them understand it was a setup?"

"Naw, I think they already know it was me done talked. I gotta get out of town."

Rachel sat up straight. "Where are you going?"

"I dunno. That was 'posed to be up to you. You done told me you'd help me get away. So it's time for you to deliver."

Rachel chewed on her lip a moment. "I can help you. I know where you can stay until we find a safe place out of town, but you've got to do something else first."

"What's that?"

"You have to meet with me. If I'm going to help you, I have to know who you are. I can't give out information about a safe house until I'm sure about you."

A sigh rippled in her ear. "Yeah. I guess it's time we met. How about the same place tonight?"

"That will be fine. But there is a condition to this." She hesitated a moment. "I'm going to bring Detective Matt Franklin from the police with me."

"What?" His yell hurt her ear and she pulled the phone away. "I ain't talkin' to no popo. I done told you they's taking payoffs."

"Detective Franklin's not. He's an honest cop, and he wants to catch this vigilante as much as we do. So you have a decision to make. Either you meet with both of us or you can find your own way out of the gang."

Rachel expected the call to disconnect but it didn't. After a moment, he spoke. "All right. I guess I ain't got no choice now. If I don't go, I gonna be killed for talking to a reporter. So I might as well talk to a cop, too."

She relaxed and flashed a victory sign at Matt. "Then we'll be waiting on the park bench tonight at midnight." The phone clicked and Rachel put the receiver back on the base. She stood up and glanced at Matt. "Want to go to meet my source tonight?"

His eyes sparkled with excitement. "That was a gutsy move, Rachel. I thought he'd hang up, but you had him hooked." His gaze drifted over her. "You're really something. You know that?"

Her face warmed. "Thank you, Matt. If we're going to catch this killer, it's going to take some aggressiveness. I thought it was time I let the source know he couldn't stay in control. Not if he's serious about getting out of the gang life. I'll call David and ask him to get a room ready at the Youth Center where he can stay until we can get him out of town."

"I have to stop by the Center on my way back to the station. I can check that out with him if you'd like."

"That would probably be better. You know he's my godfather, and he's very protective. If he knows you're going with me to the meeting, he may not be so upset."

"I'll try to put his mind at ease. I'll see you later." He headed to the door but stopped before he exited. "How about dinner tonight?"

She smiled. "That sounds great."

"Then I'll talk to you later."

Rachel nodded and sank into her desk chair. The notes she'd made while on the phone lay in front of her and she reviewed what had been said. From the beginning she'd wondered about the man with the soft voice who whispered in her ear about corruption in the police department and a killer who stalked the streets. After years in a gang, she wondered if it was possible for a person to give up the lifestyle. If things worked out tonight, she might soon have the answer to that question.

Matt stopped outside David Foreman's office at the Youth Center and knocked. When no one answered, he knocked again. He was just about to leave when David's voice rang out from down the hall.

"Matt, what are you doing here at this time of day? Aren't

you supposed to be at work? Earning the taxpayers' money, so to speak?"

Matt turned and spied David with a cup of coffee in his hand. When David stopped beside him, Matt chuckled. "I'm here about something that relates to my work. Something I hope you can help me with."

David pushed the door open. "Then come on in."

Matt followed David into the office and sat in the chair facing David's desk. David sank down, took a sip of coffee and set the cup in front of him. Folding his hands across his stomach, he studied Matt.

"Now what can I do for you?"

David pursed his lips from time to time as Matt told him about the meeting with Rachel's source and their hope that David could provide a place of safety for the gang member. "Rachel thought you have contacts that could find a place for this guy to stay for a while."

David placed his elbows on the desk and tented his fingers. "So, you're going to be with Rachel tonight?"

"Yes."

David let out a long breath and shook his head. "Then I know you'll do everything you can to protect her. Were you with her at that bar explosion the other night?"

"Yes. Did she tell you about it?"

David shook his head. "No. I read it in her column. Emily is worried sick. She's afraid Rachel has gotten in over her head."

Matt's heart thudded with the same worry. "I am, too."

"Well, you can bring the source here tonight. I'll get a room ready. And I'll start making inquiries about a permanent place. I have a friend upstate who's helped in the past. It's a rural area. Maybe he can find a place on a farm."

"Good. Rachel will be glad to hear that. I told her I'd call her later."

David regarded him with a questioning look. "Emily told

me she and Cara met you over the weekend. What did you think of them?"

Matt smiled. "I thought they were wonderful. There's a lot of love in that family."

David leaned forward. "And Cara. What did you think of her?"

Matt tilted his head and frowned. "I thought she was great. I've never seen anyone so excited over a Christmas tree. She showed me every ornament she's ever made. You know their mother keeps all of them."

"I know." David hesitated for a moment. "I'm the closest thing to a father Rachel has, and I don't want to see her get hurt. So I guess I'll just come right out and ask what I really want to know. What's going on between you and Rachel?"

The question stunned him. How could he respond when he didn't understand his own feelings, much less Rachel's? He stood and rubbed the back of his neck. "It's complicated."

David rose and faced him. "Explain that to me."

Matt's first instinct was to get out of there as quickly as he could, but David's question hammered in his thoughts. The helpless feeling that overcame him each time he thought about Rachel overtook him. He needed guidance and David might be the person to give it.

Matt took a deep breath. "All you know about me is the information I've shared when I first came here to volunteer. Maybe if you know what my past is like, you'll understand why I'm so confused."

For the next few minutes Matt poured out his anger at his parents who were never around, the money that ruled their lives, the women who'd wanted his money instead of him and his distrust of Rachel's motives in their friendship.

When he finished, he glanced at David's face. His features appeared chiseled in stone with the look he directed at Matt. "You think Rachel wants your money?"

"I don't know. She talks all the time about how she has to

get money for Cara. I don't want someone else who sees me as a meal ticket."

David studied him for a moment before he leaned forward. "Matt, it sounds like you think having money is an evil thing. The Bible says, though, that it's the love of money that is the root of evil." He hesitated a moment. "Let me ask you this. What do you do with the money you inherited from your grandfather?"

"It's invested. I don't want a penny of it. I live off what I make as a policeman."

David chuckled. "So what happens to all that wealth?"

"I have a business manager who takes care of everything. Whatever I make in a year is reinvested in other businesses."

David nodded. "So you're accumulating a lot of wealth that's just sitting out there and making more of the money you hate."

Matt's stomach roiled. "Yeah, I guess so. I've never thought of it that way."

David stood up and came around his desk. Sitting on the edge, he leaned toward Matt. "There are a lot of needs in the world. All you have to do is look around at the kids you work with here at the Center or the families of the people you arrest. People are hurting. Many don't know how they're going to pay their rent or where their next meal is coming from. Most of the kids who come to the Center live without medical insurance because their parents can't afford it. And here you are feeling sorry for yourself because you're sitting on a pile of money that just keeps getting bigger."

Matt's face grew warm. "That's not fair, David."

"Oh, it's not? I think you're living with a double standard. You don't want the money, but you don't want to give up the lifestyle it brings. If you truly hated it, you wouldn't live in a pricey condo or drive a sports car."

Matt's chest pounded at the truth in David's words. He was

a Christian. It was up to him to live his life like the example Jesus gave, not to judge others. His lips trembled. "You make me sound like a hypocrite. As a Christian, I'm supposed to be different than that."

A wry smile curled David's lips. "Being a Christian doesn't make us perfect, Matt. We all struggle with problems in our lives. When we do, we rely on God and the Christians he's placed in our lives to help us. I think you've never had anyone to guide you. Have you ever asked God to help you work out your feelings about your money?"

The question startled Matt. "Well, no. I didn't think that was important enough to bother Him."

David stared at him. "Nothing is too small for Him. Think how God has blessed you. When God gives us a gift, He doesn't expect us to keep it hidden. We're supposed to put it to work in the world. You could sure do a lot of His work if you wanted."

Matt nodded. "You're right about me, but what about Rachel? How do I find out how she feels?"

David smiled. "Rachel's past has impacted her, too. Even when she was a child, she saved half her allowance for the future. I know her heart. She sees Cara as her responsibility although Emily never intended that. As for the money part, you'll have to pray and ask God to make you understand. Look to Him for the answers you'll find in your heart."

Matt sighed and reached for David's hand. "Thank you. You've given me a lot to think about."

David shook his hand and turned back to his desk. "Anytime. That's what I'm here for."

On his way out of the building, Matt walked past the Christmas tree in the lobby. He'd helped some of the kids he worked with decorate it, but he'd never given a thought to whether or not they might have one at home.

He didn't have a tree but he knew who did. How he'd like to be a part of the Christmas celebration at the Long house where homemade ornaments decorated the tree. He'd probably spend it alone as he had so often in the past.

When he climbed behind the steering wheel, the need to hear his mother's voice overwhelmed him. Punching her number into his cell phone, he waited for her to answer. After a few rings, it went to voice mail and he ended the call.

Laying his head on the rim of the steering wheel, he prayed. "God, be with her wherever she is and let her know I do love her."

The words *peace on earth* flashed in his head, and he smiled at the happiness he'd felt watching Cara and Rachel hang their childhood ornaments on the tree. Suddenly he felt a renewed sense of hope. His mother might be like a beautiful apparition that drifted into his life from time to time, but Rachel was real. And what he felt for her was real. He didn't know if she shared his feelings but he looked forward to finding out.

THIRTEEN

The security lights scattered around the deserted park cast a glow across the snow-covered landscape. Rachel shoved her gloved hands in her coat pockets and scooted closer to Matt. Having him beside her on the bench calmed her. At least she wasn't meeting her unknown caller alone as she had done in the past.

The clock in the tower across the lake chimed the midnight hour and Matt stirred. "He should be here anytime. Are you okay?"

Rachel started to speak, but her teeth chattered. "I—I—I'm f-fine."

He turned toward her. "Scared?"

She shook her head. "No, just cold."

He raised his arm as if to put it around her shoulders but then let it drop back in his lap. Disappointment pricked Rachel's heart.

"Maybe we'll be back in the car before long." He clasped his hands in his lap and gazed at the sky. "The moon is bright tonight."

She was about to answer when a sound from behind the bench startled her. Strong fingers clamped down on her shoulder. She pulled her hand from her pocket and grasped Matt's arm.

"Hello."

"I'm here."

Rachel's body tensed. This was the moment she'd been waiting for. She was about to meet the mysterious voice in person. "I'm glad. Now I need you to come around to the front of the bench so we can see you."

Out of the corner of her eye, Rachel could see long, brown fingers on Matt's shoulder. "You ain't gonna arrest me, are you?"

"No. We want to help you. We've found a safe place for you."

Rachel held her breath and waited. A few seconds ticked by before there was movement. Then a figure emerged from the shadows to stand in front of them. He wore a heavy jacket and its hood covered his head. He reached up and pushed the hood away.

Rachel gasped in surprise. A young man, not the older hardened criminal she'd expected, stood before them. "Why, you're just a teenager."

He drew himself to his full height and gritted his teeth. "I may be young but I done lived a lot in my seventeen years."

Rachel rose and stared into his face. "What's your name?"

He glanced over his shoulder as if checking to make sure they were alone. "Edward Haines. But everybody calls me Little Eddie."

Matt stood. "How long have you been with the Vipers?"

Little Eddie glanced from Matt to Rachel. "Since I was twelve."

Rachel gasped. "Twelve years old? How did your mother feel about that?"

"Like I told you the first time we met, she ain't happy with me. That's why I came to you. Gang life ain't for me no more."

Matt took a step toward Little Eddie. "I'm happy about that. We're going to take you to the Lake City Youth Center and hide you there until the director can get you out of the city. But I need you to tell me how I can get in touch with your gang members."

Little Eddie's eyes grew wide. "Why you want to talk to them?"

"Because I've got to stop this vigilante. I don't want anybody else to be killed. Maybe if I talk to the two gangs, I can make them understand they're not fighting each other. It's someone else."

Little Eddie laughed. "Me trust the popo? I don't see that happ'nin'."

Rachel stepped forward until she was almost nose to nose with the teenager. "Now listen to me. You came to me with this story and it turned out to be the truth. The only thing we can do now is try to stop this crazy killer. You can trust Matt. He wants to do what is right. So tell him where he can meet with the Vipers."

Eddie stared at her for a few moments before he glanced at Matt. "I guess if she say you okay, that's good enough for me." He took a deep breath. "You know the One Day Dry Cleaners over on Union Street?"

Matt nodded. "Yes."

"Go in there and tell the guy behind the counter you need to meet with Shorty."

Matt glanced at Rachel and back to Little Eddie. "Should I tell him I'm a police officer or will that scare him off?"

Little Eddie smiled, revealing several missing teeth. "I 'spect you better be honest. Ain't no Viper scared of a cop but we don't like liars. So tell the guy in the cleaners who you are and what you want. It gonna be up to him whether or not you get a meeting."

"I will."

Rachel relaxed and glanced around the deserted park. "Now let's get out of here and take you to the Youth Center."

As the three of them walked toward Matt's car in the

parking lot, Rachel sneaked a sideways glance at Little Eddie from time to time. If she'd passed him on the street, she would have thought him to be a normal high school student without a worry in the world. Hidden inside him, though, were secrets of gang life and crime.

She could only hope that the chance to escape his existence would work out. Hiding him at the Center and getting him away from his former friends didn't guarantee success. It would be a struggle for the young man, but there would be help along the way. He'd brought her the biggest story of her career and she owed him. Rachel hoped what they offered him would be enough to make a difference in his life. He had a long journey toward rehabilitation ahead of him, perhaps years. She hoped he would have the strength to get through it.

Rachel sat at her desk the next morning and sipped a cup of coffee. The events of the night before replayed in her mind and she wondered how Little Eddie felt this morning. He'd been a little hesitant about Matt and her leaving him, but David had assured them he would take good care of their charge. She still couldn't get over the fact that her source had turned out to be a rather small teenager, not the husky man she'd imagined.

"Morning, Miss Long.

Rachel glanced up to see Toby standing in the doorway. He held a broom and she could see his maintenance cart in the hallway. She pushed to her feet. "Hi, Toby. Good to see you. Do you need to clean my office?"

He shook his head. "I checked it before you came in. I think the night crew did a good job. Just thought I'd see if you need your trash can emptied."

Rachel glanced at the basket beside her desk. "It's okay."

Toby backed out of the room. "See you later."

The ringing of her cell phone interrupted her response

to Toby. She pulled the phone from her purse and smiled at Matt's name on the caller ID. "Good morning, Matt."

"Hi, Rachel." His voice set her pulse to racing and she smiled. "I wanted to check in with you and see how you made it after last night."

"I'm fine. I can't wait for our meeting with the Vipers. When are we going?"

"Now wait a minute." The exasperation in his voice wiped the smile from her face. "This time you aren't going. This is police work and I'm not taking you."

She sprang to her feet and pounded her fist on the desk. "Now you listen to me, Matt Franklin. This is my story. You wouldn't even have met Little Eddie if it hadn't been for me. I was the one who made him tell you where you could meet the head of the Vipers. I know where the One Day Dry Cleaners on Union is, and I can go there without you, too. Do you want me to beat you to the visit?"

A sigh rippled in her ear. "No, I don't. But I think this is too dangerous for you."

She shook her head as she paced back and forth across her office. "It's not, and I intend to be there with or without you. Now which is it going to be?"

"All right. I guess I can't fight you on this one. You sure are a stubborn woman."

She smiled. "So you've said before. Now tell me when you'll pick me up for the meeting."

"I thought I'd go after lunch. How about if I come by your office about one-thirty?"

"Sounds good to me. I'll be ready."

"I'll see you then."

Rachel ended the call and walked back to her desk. She tossed her cell phone on her desk and it jarred the cup of coffee she'd set there earlier. Startled, she reached for the cup but only succeeded in knocking it over. She grabbed her cell phone before it could get wet, but the coffee puddle spread across the desk and dripped to the floor.

Pulling a handful of tissues from a box at the edge of her desk, she mopped at the mess on her desk. The tissues soon disintegrated in the large pool of coffee. She would have to get something from Toby to clean this mess.

Rachel rushed from her office and hurried to Toby's maintenance room at the end of the hall. She knocked at the closed door but no one answered. A glance up and down the hall didn't reveal Toby or his cart.

Rachel pushed the door open and peeked inside. "Toby, are you here?"

Silence greeted her as she stepped inside the cluttered room. Brooms and mops hung on pegs around the wall and gallon containers of cleaning materials sat stacked atop each other. Rachel wriggled between several boxes of paper towels and reached for a mop on a peg beside Toby's desk.

She grabbed the mop and pulled it toward her. As she started to back away, she glanced down and her breath caught in her throat. Unable to move, she stared at an open catalog on Toby's desk. She glanced over her shoulder before she inched forward until she could determine if she was really seeing what she thought.

Rachel reached out and picked up the magazine. Her eyes grew larger as she thumbed through the pages that advertised the latest in guns and ammunition. She turned back to the page with the turned-down corner she had first seen. Several high-powered rifles displayed turned her blood cold. But it was the one with a big circle around it that shocked her the most. Next to the picture someone had written the words "buy this one."

Why was Toby buying a rifle like this? One with a scope for long-distance shooting. She dropped the magazine on the desk and covered her mouth with her hand. The sniper would want a gun like this.

With the mop in hand she hurried to the door and into the hall. She looked around but no one appeared to notice her leaving the room. As she hurried back to her office, her mind whirled. What had she found? Was Toby the sniper? Was he the one who had told her he was going to kill her?

She rushed into her office and closed the door. Leaning against the wood panel, she tried to collect her thoughts. The sniper had called her on her cell phone. With a sinking heart she realized her cell phone number was available to any of the newspaper staff. That wouldn't have been hard for Toby to discover. But could the gentle man she'd known for the past year be a killer?

She glanced around her office and her skin tingled at something Toby had said earlier about checking out her office. How had he done that? The door had been locked when she arrived at work. The answer hit her and she groaned. Toby had a key to all the offices.

He stepped into the cold morning air and headed for his car in the parking lot. Nobody would miss him from work for a few minutes while he checked his phone for any calls Rachel Long had made or received. If anyone noticed him, he would say he was looking for something he thought he left in the car.

He climbed in behind the steering wheel and slid down in the seat so that his head was barely visible to anyone outside. His eyes lit with excitement at the messages from Rachel's phone.

He listened to one after another that had recorded on his phone this morning. He waited patiently as he heard her conversations with her mother, her best friend Mindy and the receptionist at her favorite hair salon. With one more to go, he didn't expect much, but he jerked to attention at the call from Matt Franklin.

He listened with growing concern as they discussed her

source that was now hiding at the Lake City Youth Center. He gritted his teeth and clenched his fists at the memory of the Viper who got away that night in front of the pizza parlor. At least now he knew his name and where he was hiding. Little Eddie was one more name to add to his list.

It was the last of the conversation that really excited him. He listened with rapt attention as Matt and Rachel argued over whether or not she should go with him to a meeting with the head of the Vipers. He chuckled when Rachel won out. That suited him just fine.

When the call ended, he closed his phone and thought about what he should do. Opportunities like this didn't present themselves every day. He couldn't let Rachel and Matt have all the fun. He'd have to crash their little party and make sure it was one they'd never forget. That is, if they lived to tell about it.

Laughing to himself, he climbed from the car and headed back inside. He could hardly wait to see Rachel and Matt at the One Day Dry Cleaner this afternoon. It should be a memorable meeting.

Matt pulled into a parking place on Commerce Street around the corner from the dry cleaner. Next to him, Rachel looked tense with her hands clasped in her lap. He wished she wasn't with him, and he'd tried to keep her away. Knowing how determined she could be, he supposed it was better to have her close where he could keep an eye on her than to attempt to confront the leader of the Vipers alone.

She glanced over at him. Her face didn't convey her usual self-control. Her lips flashed a weak smile and her chin trembled slightly as she spoke. "Well, I guess this is it."

"Yeah. I guess so." He swiveled in his seat to face her. "It's not too late to change your mind. I'll tell you everything that happens if you want to stay in the car."

She shook her head. "I have to see this thing through, Matt.

I've had a death threat, my apartment has been broken into, I've been followed by someone in a beat-up car and now the custodian that I trust is buying high-powered rifles. I've got to find out what's going on."

He laid his arm on the back of her seat. He wanted to grasp her shoulders and pull her closer for protection but he didn't. "You're still upset over the incident with Toby this morning. Maybe you shouldn't go with me."

Rachel pulled her gloves from her coat pocket and slipped them on. She tried to steady her hands but he saw the tremble. "I'm not staying behind."

Matt flexed his fingers as he pulled his arm away and reached for the door handle. "Then let's go see if we can get the guy in the cleaners to set up a meeting for us."

He stepped onto the pavement and waited for her to join him. As they started up the sidewalk, he studied her out of the corner of his eye. She might be scared but to anyone else it probably wasn't visible. She looked every inch the determined investigator. He admired her for being able to project that appearance when he knew all that happened in the past few days had taken a toll on her emotions.

When they rounded the corner onto Union Avenue, people clustered at the corner waiting for the light to change so they could cross. Matt glanced up and down the sidewalk crowded with pedestrians. With a college two blocks from this part of the city, quite a few trendy shops and restaurants had opened in the area. Every time he drove down Union, he was shocked at how this section of the inner city was reinventing itself.

He took Rachel's arm as they worked their way through the people and leaned toward her. "There's a lot of people on the streets today."

She glanced up at him and pointed to the sale sign in a boutique window. "They're Christmas shoppers out to get bargains. I saw all the ads in this morning's paper."

A woman carrying a huge shopping bag in each hand

barreled toward them as if oblivious to those around her. Matt let go of Rachel's arm and the woman walked between them without taking notice of either one.

When she'd passed, they stopped and stared in her direction. Matt shook his head. "She looks like she's on a mission."

Rachel chuckled and pointed to a store across the street where a group of people were entering. "Maybe she's going over there. They must have a big sale...."

Matt glanced at Rachel, but she didn't move. Her gaze appeared locked across the street on the store with sports apparel displayed in the window. He touched her arm. "Rachel, what's the matter?"

Without a word, Rachel bolted into the street in front of an oncoming car. The vehicle squealed to a halt. Matt ran in front of it in pursuit of Rachel. The driver rolled his window down and shook his fist. "Watch out where you're going!"

Matt turned and waved to him. "Sorry."

He caught up with Rachel at the sidewalk curb and grabbed her arm. Jerking her around, he stared into her wide eyes. "What's the matter with you? You almost got killed."

She pulled away from him and pointed toward the store. "Toby just went inside that store. What's he doing on the street where we're going to meet the Vipers?"

Matt reached inside his jacket and touched the gun in his shoulder holster. "I don't know but I think we'd better find out."

The revolver seemed to heat up and spread its warmth through his shirt to his skin. Matt tensed. Toby had looked harmless enough when he saw him at the newspaper office, but you could never tell what went on inside another person's mind. It was always better to be prepared. He touched the gun again, frowned and pulled his hand out of his jacket. Drawing his weapon in the middle of a crowded store could lead to disaster.

His heart beat out a tattoo as he stepped through the door of the sporting-goods store and let his gaze sweep the shoppers. The mass of bodies in front of him concealed a man who had a penchant for high-powered rifles as did the vigilante. Before he could blink, he and Rachel could be cut down by gunfire and left to die in the middle of screaming holiday shoppers.

He glanced over his shoulder and motioned for her to stay behind him. Leading the way, Matt inched forward and began his search for the *Daily Beacon*'s custodian.

FOURTEEN

Rachel stayed behind Matt as they stepped into the customers crowded around display tables at the front of the store. The ad in the morning newspaper had attracted a lot of attention from the looks of the shoppers. Matt squeezed between two women rifling through sweatshirts with professional football insignia and another examining a display of hooded pullovers. Rachel stopped to keep from running into a man who darted into her path and lost sight of Matt.

Pushing through the shoppers, she spotted him down an aisle with boxes of tennis shoes on either side and hurried to catch up. He glanced over his shoulder as she stopped and asked, "Do you see him?"

Matt shook his head and walked to the end of the aisle, then started up another. "There's a lot of people in here."

"Maybe we need to split up. I'll call you if I spot him and you can do the same."

"All right. If we don't find him, we'll meet out front in fifteen minutes."

"Okay."

Rachel walked back to the middle aisle of the store and began a sweep of the area. Every person she saw appeared intent on studying the sales items and paid her no attention. Hoping to blend into the crowd, she sauntered up one aisle and then another, but Toby was nowhere to be seen.

After fifteen minutes of searching, she pushed back through the crowd and stepped onto the sidewalk. She glanced up and down the street, but Toby had disappeared.

Matt emerged from the store and joined her. "Did you see him?"

"No, it was like the crowd swallowed him up. Did you?"

"No." Matt glanced back at the store. "Maybe he went out the back before we got inside. He could be anywhere. I think we should give up on Toby and go on to the dry cleaners."

The business sat across the street from where they stood. A young man wearing a football letterman jacket from the college nearby emerged from inside. He carried several pieces of clothing on hangers. Rachel tilted her head to one side and watched the young man get into a parked car. "It doesn't look like a place that would be involved with gang activity."

"Most of them don't." Matt took a deep breath. "Well, let's go see what we can do."

They stopped at the front door of the One Day Dry Cleaners. Matt pulled it open and stepped back for Rachel to enter first. Together they approached the counter.

A young man with bushy hair and the name *Lauren* tattooed in large letters on the side of his neck looked up from the cash register as they approached. His gaze swept their hands. "Are you picking up cleaning?"

Matt shook his head and pulled out his badge. "I'm Detective Matt Franklin with the Lake City Police Department. We're here on other business."

The young man glanced from the badge to Rachel. "You a cop, too?"

"No, my name is Rachel Long. I'm a reporter with the *Daily Beacon*."

His facial expression revealed no hint of recognizing either one of them. "So what can I do for you?"

Matt shoved his badge back in his pocket and stared at the

man. "You probably know there've been some shootings on the street lately with a lot of gang members being killed."

"I heard something about that."

"The police thought the Vipers and the Rangers were trying to kill each other off until Miss Long here discovered there was a vigilante who wanted to provoke a gang war."

The man's gaze flickered toward Rachel. "Yeah, I heard about that, too."

Matt leaned forward. "I want to stop this guy before that happens. I need to make sure nobody gets nervous and makes a hit on the other gang before we can catch this vigilante."

The man shrugged. "So, dude, what you want me to do about it? I just run a dry cleaners."

Matt didn't break eye contact with him. "I know you can get word to Shorty. Tell him we want to meet with him. Today."

A smile cracked the man's face. "What makes you think I know anybody called Shorty?"

Rachel stepped up to the counter. "Please. We need your help. This vigilante is going to keep killing until he's stopped. Get word to the Vipers. I know they've read my stories. Tell them they can trust me and they can trust Matt. David Foreman will vouch for both of us."

His forehead wrinkled. "You know Mr. Foreman?"

"He's my godfather. Will you help us?"

The man glanced from one to another before he shrugged. "I'll see what I can do, but I don't promise nothing. Wait here."

He walked to the front door, locked it and turned a sign that hung in the middle of the glass from the Open side to Closed. Walking past them, he disappeared through a door into the back of the building. Rachel turned to Matt. "What do you think?"

"I don't know. We'll see."

The minutes ticked by as they waited. Rachel paced back and forth, glancing at her watch from time to time. After fifteen minutes, the door the man had entered reopened and he motioned for them to follow.

Rachel followed Matt into a darkened room. She blinked as her eyes adjusted to the dim light. In front of her Matt hesitated before he took a step forward. She heard the click of the door and looked over her shoulder. The man from the dry cleaners had followed them, closed the door and now stood beside it with his arms crossed. The expression on his face sent tremors of fear through her. She stepped up beside Matt and peered at the man who sat alone at a table in the rear of the room.

To Rachel, he didn't look very different from many of the young men she'd seen on the streets of Lake City, but she sensed something in his attitude that chilled her blood. He wore the same colors she'd seen on three of the murder victims and recognized them as the mark of a Viper. He sat with his chair leaned on its hind legs, one arm draped over the back.

His eyes narrowed as they approached. "Come on in and have a seat. I ain't gonna hurt you. You the ones wantin' this meetin'."

Matt pulled out a chair for Rachel and sat in the one next to it. "I understand they call you Shorty. Thank you for meeting with us. I know your time's valuable and I don't want to take up too much of it."

The Viper gave a slight nod. Rachel remembered what Matt had told her about treating gang members with respect. This man appeared to expect it. He glanced from Matt to Rachel. "What can I do for you?"

Rachel listened as Matt related the stories she had written, how they were shot at by the vigilante and how they witnessed the explosion at Pepper's Bar. When he finished, he sat back in his chair. "We hope you believe what we've discovered about this vigilante, and we want to ask you not to take any aggressive measures against the Rangers. They aren't responsible for your members' deaths."

When Matt finished speaking, Shorty pulled a quarter from his pocket and began to flip it up and down in his palm. He didn't speak for a few minutes. Then he glanced up at Rachel. "I been readin' those stories in the paper and I think you right. But I got some upset brothers. They ready for some revenge."

Rachel swallowed and hoped her words would come from her now dry throat. "I understand, but there's no need for that. If you kill a Ranger, they're going to retaliate. Then are you any better off? All we're asking is that you get word to the Rangers that you want a truce until the police can find out who's behind all these murders."

He stared at Rachel before he pushed to his feet. "I ain't gonna promise nothing. But I'll talk to my brothers. Maybe we can hold off for a little while."

Matt stood and Rachel rose to stand beside him. Matt stared at Shorty. "I hope you're successful."

Shorty motioned to the man who still stood by the door that led into the dry cleaners. He left his post and hurried across the room and unlocked the back door.

Rachel smiled and waved to Shorty. "Thank you for meeting with us."

Shorty stepped outside and turned to wave just before the sharp crack of a rifle echoed down the alley where he stood. Rachel watched in horror as he spun around and fell facedown in the street. Beside her Matt whipped out his gun and sprinted to the back door, but the man from the dry cleaners had already pulled a gun from his pocket and rushed outside. Another shot ripped the air and he fell forward over his friend.

"Get down!"

Matt's scream propelled Rachel downward. Her fingernails clawed at the floor underneath her. She peeked up to see Matt crouching at the back door, his phone to his ear. She heard him calling for help, but she jammed her hands over her ears as another shot struck the side of the building.

Near her the report of another gun exploded. Matt was exchanging fire with the shooter. Once again she was reminded of the dangers that policemen faced each day and she was terrified for Matt's safety.

The shooting ceased. The silence scared her more than the gunfire. The thought that Matt might be hit forced her to her feet. She could hear the sirens of approaching police cars. Rushing to the closed back door, she opened it and peered into the alley. Matt leaned over the two bodies. He glanced up and saw her in the doorway.

He stood and came toward her. "You need to stay inside."

She backed into the room and he followed. Rachel looked up at him and tears gushed from her eyes. He smiled and wiped at them with his thumb. "It's over. You're safe."

Her heart burst with relief that he was alive, and she threw her arms around him and clung with all her might. He stiffened for a moment, then relaxed. His arms circled her back and drew her closer.

Rachel just wanted to hold him and know that he was all right. "I was so scared. I thought you'd been shot, too. I couldn't stand it if something happened to you."

"I'm okay, Rachel." His breath fanned her ear. She clung to him for a few more moments before he gently pushed her away. "I have to go outside. Will you be all right here?"

She shook her head. "No, I'll go with you. After all, this is a story and I need to cover it."

Before he could respond, the back door opened and Philip stuck his head inside. "Hey, partner, we have a crime scene out here. Are you coming to help?"

Matt smiled at Rachel and inclined his head in Philip's direction. "Duty calls."

She wiped at the tears on her face and turned toward the door. She really didn't want to see the bodies in the alley. A few minutes ago, she was talking to the two men who now lay dead a few feet away.

It wouldn't take long for word of their deaths to reach the Vipers, and they might begin plotting a revenge that could engulf the city in an all-out street war. She had to make sure that didn't happen. Her story might be the only thing that could stop it. She was a reporter and right now she had a job to do.

Straightening her shoulders and taking a deep breath, she turned from Matt and strode toward the back door. She pushed away the fears that had attacked her earlier, stepped into the alley and pulled her notepad from her purse.

Hours later, Matt sat in his office filling out the reports on the deaths of the two gang members. He let the pen drop from his fingers, propped his elbows on the desk and raked his fingers through his hair. He couldn't forget the look on Rachel's face when she peered into the alley and saw him bending over the bodies.

The way she shook when she clung to him had puzzled him at first. Then his heart had pounded like an anvil when he realized she was scared for him. Her words still echoed in his mind. *I couldn't stand it if something happened to you.* Did she really mean it?

The door opened. He straightened as Philip walked into the office. He stopped in front of Matt's desk. "You okay, buddy?"

Matt nodded and picked up the pen. "Yeah, just thinking about the crime scene. You'd think after a while I'd get used to it, but I never have."

Philip dropped the papers he held on his desk and leaned against the edge of it. He crossed his arms and exhaled. "I know. I've forgotten how many crime scenes I've been to in my fifteen years of police work, but it never gets any better. Every time it's like I'm seeing one for the first time."

Matt rose and walked to the one window in the room and stared outside to the parking lot. "Me, too. I guess this one today was worse because I had just finished talking to those guys."

"That's what you said. It was a good try to make some peace between the two gangs, Matt, but after what happened I'm afraid it's not going to work."

Matt sighed and turned back to his desk. "I think you're probably right."

Philip straightened and walked over to Matt. He balled his fist and gave Matt a playful punch on the shoulder. "Come on, man, we'll catch this guy. It's just going to take us some time. Until we do, you have other things to concentrate on."

"Like what?"

Philip's eyebrows arched and he chuckled. "Don't pretend you don't understand. I saw how you looked at that newspaper reporter and how she looked at you when you weren't watching."

Matt's face grew warm. He ducked his head and reached for the report on his desk. "She did?"

Philip stepped over and took the papers from his hand. "Yeah. It's obvious there's something going on between the two of you." He glanced at his watch. "It's almost quitting time. Why don't you let me finish these reports and you go check on her. See how she's feeling. Maybe take her out to dinner. Besides, I have to record my conversation with that custodian at the paper."

"I really appreciate you taking care of that while I was finishing up at the dry cleaners." Matt glanced at the papers Philip held. "But I hate to leave you with this."

Philip laughed and shook his head. "I'm just glad to be back at work today. I don't mind. Now go on."

Matt grabbed his coat from the rack by the door and pulled it on. "Thanks, Philip. I'll pay you back for this."

Philip had already sat down at his desk and waved. "Get out of here. I'll see you tomorrow."

Fifteen minutes later Matt stopped at Rachel's open office door and peered inside. She sat at her desk and appeared to be concentrating on something on her computer screen. For a moment all he wanted to do was stare at her. He should have known the first time he looked into her blue eyes that he was in trouble, but he'd resisted. Now he couldn't deny it any longer, he'd never felt about any woman the way he felt for Rachel.

He still hadn't come to grips with his reservations about Rachel's true feelings, but her words at the crime scene had given him hope. All he could do was to follow David's advice. He had to put their relationship in God's hands. Then he would know if he should trust his head or his heart.

A movement at the door caught her attention, and Rachel glanced up from the computer. At the sight of Matt, her heart squeezed with the fear she'd now experienced twice—once when he was hurt at Pepper's Bar and today when she feared he'd been shot. The memory of her words to him made her skin warm.

She smiled and stood. "Matt, what are you doing here?"

He sauntered into the room and she clutched the side of her desk to keep from running toward him. It had felt so good when he had his arms around her today, but she needed to remind herself he would have done the same to any witness at a murder scene. He stopped in front of her. "I thought we might grab a bite to eat."

Disappointment washed over her. "I would love to but I can't."

He blinked and the expression on his face darkened. "That's okay. Maybe another time. I'll talk to you tomorrow."

He turned toward the door, but she rushed around the desk

and grabbed his arm. "Wait, don't run off. You didn't let me finish."

Her fingers tightened on his arm as he faced her. "What?"

Rachel relaxed her grip and smiled. "I was going to tell you that my mother called and wants me to come to dinner there. I know she and Cara would love to see you again."

He shook his head. "Your mother's not expecting me and I wouldn't want to impose."

Rachel laughed. "Impose on my mother? If I know her, she's cooked up enough for me to carry leftovers home. You'll save me a lot of repetitive meals this next week if you'll eat part of it."

He smiled and her heart pounded. "In that case, I'd love to go. I need to check on our tree anyway and see if Cara's taking care of it."

Rachel hurried back to her desk and pulled her cell phone from her purse. "I'll call Mama and tell her to set another plate."

Her mother answered on the first ring. "Hello."

"Hey, Mama. I thought I'd give you notice that I'm bringing someone home for dinner."

A chuckled rattled in her ear. "I hope it's Matt. Cara's asked a dozen times today when he was coming back."

Rachel smiled. "Yes, it's Matt. So set an extra plate."

"I will. See you later."

A wave of happiness washed over Rachel as she ended the call and bent over her computer. "Let me turn this off and I'll be ready to go."

As she reached to close out the email she'd been reading, she remembered what she'd been pondering when Matt walked into her office. She reread the message Cal had sent out to all the employees that afternoon and bit her lip. Glancing at Matt, she pasted a smile on her face that she hoped hid the uncertainty she felt.

"As long as I'm extending invitations to you, how about one more?"

He cocked an eyebrow. "What kind of invitation?"

She pointed to the computer. "When you came in, I was reading the final arrangements for the newspaper's Christmas party for employees. It's Friday night at the Stargazer Ballroom. I'd love for you to go as my guest."

His eyes twinkled. "Are you asking me out on a date, Miss Long?"

Her pulse raced at the smile he directed toward her. "I suppose I am, Mr. Franklin."

"In that case, I'd be honored to be your escort to the Christmas party."

"Then let me reply to this message that I'm bringing a guest. They're trying to get a count for dinner."

She sank into her chair, typed her response and hit Send. When she glanced up, Matt was studying her with an intense stare. His gaze appeared riveted to her lips and she wondered what it would feel like to experience his kiss. With shaking fingers she turned off the computer and took a deep breath.

Rachel hadn't lost the cheerful feeling Matt's presence had brought when they walked from her office a few minutes later. He brushed against her arm as he pushed the down button for the elevator, and a tremor of pleasure surged through her.

As they stepped into the elevator, she glanced down the hall and spied Toby Jones standing next to his maintenance cart outside her office. His penetrating stare evaporated the joy of a few minutes before and she took a step back. As the door closed, she caught a last glimpse of him entering her office.

Beside her, Matt frowned. "What's the matter?"

"I saw Toby going into my office." She struggled to voice the question she'd wanted to ask Matt ever since the shooting. "Do you think he killed those two men today?"

Matt thought for a moment before he replied, "We didn't

find any evidence that he was at the crime scene, but then we really didn't find anything. All I know at this point is that Toby was in the neighborhood, which casts suspicion on him, but we can't connect him to the murders. Philip came by and questioned him earlier."

The news surprised Rachel. "I didn't know that. What did Toby say?"

"That he took a late lunch and went Christmas shopping. He said he saw an ad in the morning newspaper for some shirts, but when he got there, they'd all been sold. And we do know there were a lot of shoppers in that store."

Rachel thought back to their search of the store. She knew they had covered the entire place without seeing him anywhere. "He could have spotted us and ducked out the back door. He had plenty of time to get in position for the shooting. Can't you arrest him on suspicion of murder?"

"Not without proof."

Rachel sighed. "I know you're right. I guess I was just hoping. You will be watching him, won't you?"

"Oh, yeah. After this afternoon, he went to the top of my list as the suspect. Have you thought about whether or not he might have been the Santa who stole your purse?"

"I've thought about it. It's possible, I suppose."

The door opened and they stepped into the lobby. Matt turned to her. "Then I'll warn you again to be careful. Until we catch this vigilante, don't trust anybody." He took her arm and started toward the door but stopped and looked at her. "Are you back in your apartment?"

"Yes. The superintendent changed the locks."

Matt nodded. "Then I'll follow you home. I want you to leave your car there and ride with me to your mother's house. I'll bring you home later and make sure you get in safely."

"Thanks, Matt. I appreciate it."

They stepped into the late afternoon shadows and headed toward the parking lot. Her gaze darted across the nearby buildings and at the street where the Santa had run the day of the theft. The vigilante could be hiding anywhere with his gun trained on them right now. The thought almost paralyzed her with fear.

She wanted this nightmare to be over. She wanted her life back.

Matt's grip on her arm tightened and she glanced down at his fingers. No, she didn't want her old life back. She wanted a new one that included Matt Franklin, but he'd given her no sign that their relationship would continue after this case was solved.

And should it continue? After the rejections she'd received from her father and Justin, she didn't want to open herself up to that kind of hurt again. Perhaps it was better if they didn't see each other after the vigilante was caught.

Her responsibility to Cara's future had always been the most important thing for her, and she needed to remember that. She couldn't be selfish and want something for herself. She shook her head and blinked back tears. She'd never known caring for a man could produce so many problems.

FIFTEEN

Dinner had gone well. Rachel put the last plate in the dishwasher and glanced around the kitchen for anything she'd missed. Cara had been thrilled to have Matt back for a visit, and Matt appeared to enjoy all the attention Cara lavished on him throughout the meal. She'd never seen her sister so taken with anyone. Even better than that was the fact that she'd never had one of her male friends act as if he really liked Cara.

Rachel turned back to the sink and pulled the dishwashing detergent from underneath. Footsteps tapped across the floor behind Rachel. She smiled at the sight of her mother entering the room.

"Rachel, you didn't have to clean the kitchen. I got to talking to Matt and stayed in the living room longer than I meant."

Rachel turned back to the dishwasher and poured the detergent in the receptacle. "Oh? You weren't showing him my baby pictures, were you?"

Her mother laughed and sat down in a chair at the kitchen table. "No. I asked him about his family."

Rachel's eyes grew wide and she plopped down opposite her mother. "He's told me a few things about his parents. What did he tell you?"

Her mother shrugged. "Just that he doesn't see them often. Evidently he comes from a very wealthy family."

"I know. What else did he say?"

"Well, he talked quite a bit about his church and his beliefs." Her mother reached across the table and squeezed Rachel's arm. "He's a believer, Rachel. Not like all the other men you've brought home. I think Matt's a keeper."

Rachel folded the dish towel she held and laid it on the table. "You know I haven't had much time for God or church lately. So the fact that he's a believer really doesn't matter to me."

Her mother's gasp made her heart lurch. She had hoped they wouldn't get off on her mother's favorite topic tonight, but here they were discussing it again.

"I can't believe you'd say that. I pray every night that you are going to wake up and see how much God loves you. He's sent you this wonderful man who wants to share the joy of being a believer with you. Matt told me he's been trying to get you to join their Bible study."

"He has. But I don't have time to do that. I'm volunteering with David at the Center. That takes up enough of my time." Rachel shook her head. "Besides, Matt and I are just friends. I can't be involved with any man, Mama."

Surprise flashed across her mother's face. "What does that mean?"

Rachel grasped her hands in her lap and took a deep breath. "I have Cara to think about. Someday you may not be here. Then I'll be all that Cara has. I have to make sure that she'll be cared for in the future."

Her mother closed her eyes and shook her head. "Oh, Rachel. Since you were a child, you've believed that Cara was your responsibility. But you can't put your life on hold for what may never happen." She stood, came around the table and knelt by Rachel's chair. Clasping Rachel's hand, she stared into her eyes. "You deserve to love and to be loved."

Tears trickled down Rachel's face. "I love Cara with all my heart and I want to do what's best for her."

Her mother's hand tightened. "You can do that by opening up your eyes to what God has planned for you. God loves you, Rachel, but He loves Cara, too, and He's going to take care of both my girls. Just trust Him. I know He's going to send you a man who has the strength of character to look beneath the surface and see what's really important, and Matt may be the one."

Rachel hugged her mother. "Let's not talk about this tonight. It's almost Christmas and I want this to be special for Cara."

"I want it to be special for both of you." Her mother rose and kissed the top of Rachel's head. "Now dry those eyes and get in the living room. I think Matt needs to be rescued. He's probably had to read Cara her favorite book three or four times by now."

Rachel laughed and wiped the tears from her face. She wished she could confide in her mother how much Matt had come to mean to her but she couldn't. Rachel knew there was no use in getting her hopes up. She'd been disappointed in the past and she might be again.

An hour later, Rachel snuggled back in the rich leather seat of Matt's car and sighed. She didn't know when she'd enjoyed an evening more. The meal, the Christmas decorations in the house and being with people she loved had made it a time she wouldn't forget.

"Are you warm enough?" Matt's voice cut into the silence. He'd been quiet on most of the ride and she'd been content to bask in her private thoughts.

She sat up straighter. "I'm fine. I was thinking about the evening. I hope Cara didn't tire you out. When she finds someone who'll read to her, she won't leave them alone."

He chuckled. "I enjoyed it even though I did get a little tired about the fifth time through the book."

Rachel laughed. "I understand. She usually drafts me for the job. Thanks for filling in for me tonight."

"No problem. I really enjoyed it."

Rachel thought back to what her mother had said earlier. Could Matt see beneath the surface to Cara's beautiful soul and accept her or was he only being a polite guest in their home? She needed the answer to that question.

Her cell phone rang and she fished it out of her bag. She hoped Cal wasn't calling with a late-night assignment. She put the phone to her ear.

"Hello."

"Did you enjoy the evening at your mother's house?"

Rachel stiffened and swiveled toward Matt. "Who is this?"

The laugh she'd come to know drifted into her ear and chilled her blood. "You know who this is, Rachel. By this time I feel like we're old friends."

"How did you know I was at my mother's house?" Her voice grew shrill.

"I know everything about you. I'm watching you. I've also got my eye on your mother and sister."

Matt gripped the steering wheel and leaned closer. "Is that the vigilante?"

Rachel nodded.

"Keep him talking until I can stop."

She could hardly hold the phone still for her shaking hand. "What about my mother and sister?"

"I'd hate to see anything happen to them. Wouldn't you?"

The evil words meant to scare her had the opposite effect. Anger surged through her and she gripped the phone tighter. "Now you listen to me, you're a murderer and a coward who kills from a hiding place. You can't scare me because your time is about up. The police are closer than you think."

"Oh, really?"

Matt swerved into the parking lot of an all-night convenience store and skidded to a stop. Grabbing the phone from Rachel, he jammed it to his ear. "What do you want?" Rachel leaned closer hoping to hear the caller's answer. Matt frowned. "Answer me. What do you want?"

After a moment he handed the phone back to Rachel. "He hung up. What did he say?"

Rachel clutched the phone in her hand and squeezed it as she recalled his words. "He threatened my mother and sister." She grabbed Matt's arm. "Do you think they're in danger?"

Matt shook his head and pulled his cell phone from the clip on his belt. "I don't know. I'll call dispatch and have them send patrol cars by the house on a regular basis tonight."

As Matt made the call, Rachel closed her eyes and concentrated on the voice of the vigilante. Although she didn't recognize it, there was something familiar in the way he spoke. After several seconds, she opened her eyes. It was no use. She had no idea who he was. All she could do was hope that her mother and sister wouldn't be harmed because of the story she thought would move her up the ladder to success.

Matt paced back and forth across the office he shared with Philip. He couldn't shake the memory of the fear he'd seen in Rachel's face last night. "He threatened her mother and sister, Philip. They're two of the gentlest souls I've ever met. What kind of monster would threaten innocent people like that?"

Philip, who'd sat silent while Matt poured out the events of the previous evening, stood and came around his desk. "I don't know, Matt. This guy already has a long list of victims. He killed an innocent guy at Pepper's Bar, so maybe he doesn't care."

"But I don't understand that. A woman and her special-needs daughter? We've got to find him before anybody else gets hurt."

Philip picked up a folder from his desk and thumbed

through it. He stopped at the picture of the firebombing at the bar. "The list of victims keeps getting longer, but we haven't found anything that will lead us to the killer." He bit down on his lip and closed the folder. "That is, if there is a vigilante. We're taking the word of a gang member who could be trying to throw suspicion off his brothers. Have you thought about that?"

"I have, but I changed my mind after I met him."

Philip's eyes widened and he tossed the folder on his desk. "You haven't told me anything about that. When did it happen?"

Matt winced at the accusing attitude of Philip's words. Partners shouldn't keep anything from each other. "I'm sorry I haven't told you. It happened a few nights ago. I've been so distracted with the things happening to Rachel. And then with you out sick, I just forgot to tell you."

"I understand. Tell me what happened."

For the next few minutes Matt related the events of the meeting with Little Eddie. When he finished, Philip sat down on the edge of his desk and exhaled. "It sounds like you've had a busy few days. So you think Rachel's source is going to be safe at the Center?"

"David will see that no one knows he's there and I'll check in on him now and then. And so will Rachel. She's volunteering there now."

Philip stood and stretched. "If you need any help, let me know. I could drop by, too, and see if he needs anything."

Matt shook his head. "Thanks, but that won't be necessary. At this point I think the fewer people he sees, the better. He's just a scared kid, and he wants out of the gang life."

"Well, maybe this is one kid we can save. But there are a lot more of them on the streets." Philip picked up the empty coffee cup on his desk. "I'm going to the break room for coffee. Do you want me to bring you a cup?"

"No, thanks. I think I'll call Rachel and see how she's making it this morning."

A smile spread across Philip's face. "I never thought I'd see it but you've got it bad, buddy. Give Rachel my best."

As Philip walked from the room, Matt replayed his words. Got it bad? Was it really so evident to everyone around him that he was becoming more attached to Rachel every day? Attached wasn't the right word and he knew it. He had to come to grips with the war that waged inside of him. The uncertainty of what Rachel wanted from him was tearing him apart.

He didn't have a clue how she felt, but right now it didn't matter. If he was going to get on with his day, he had to hear her voice. He picked up his cell phone and punched in her number.

SIXTEEN

Rachel had attended the annual Christmas party alone ever since she came to the newspaper. This year was different. Matt was beside her as they entered the Stargazer Ballroom. She slipped her arm through his and paused at the door to take in the decorated wonderland before them.

Christmas wreaths hung from every door into the ballroom, and arrangements of red and white carnations with candy canes stuck between the flowers graced the white-draped tables. At one end of the room a round framework with circular shelves held hundreds of potted poinsettias to form a tree of the Christmas blooms that reached toward the ceiling. At the opposite end, white lights, red mercury ornaments and swirls of tinsel graced the branches of a spruce tree she judged to be perhaps twelve feet high. The strains of Christmas carols drifted from the string quartet beside the decorated tree.

Rachel closed her eyes and inhaled the smells of Christmas—the pine from the boughs on the window sills, the scent of vanilla drifting from the lit candles scattered about and the enticing aroma of the hams and turkeys waiting to be carved at the serving stations. The familiar odors evoked memories of past Christmases. She glanced at Matt. This Christmas she had someone new to help her celebrate and share the holiday.

Tonight she wanted to forget gangs and the vigilante who

stalked their streets. There had been no more calls from the killer after the one she'd received on the way home from her mother's house a few nights earlier and she'd begun to breathe a little easier. If his goal had been to scare her, he'd succeeded. But she wasn't going to let it interfere with this night.

Cal Belmont spotted them and came across the dining room to meet them. Cal, who always had his shirt collar unbuttoned and his sleeves rolled up to his elbows, looked very different tonight in his white dinner jacket. Rachel pulled her arm free and waved to Cal's wife, who she was sure was responsible for his transformation, before she leaned closer to Matt. "Here comes my editor. Have you ever met him?"

Before she could answer, Cal stopped in front of them. "Rachel, welcome. And you've brought a guest. I don't think we've met. I'm Cal Belmont."

Cal stuck out his hand and the two men shook. "I'm Matt Franklin, a friend of Rachel's."

"Well, glad you could join us tonight, Matt." He turned to Rachel. "I think your table is near the buffet. The staff tells me they're about ready to begin serving, so you'd better get seated."

Rachel led the way across the room, sidestepping the tables that dotted the area. She'd almost reached her destination when she glanced to the side and spotted Toby. His hands were shoved in his pockets and he directed a glare at her that sent goose bumps up her spine. Her foot caught on a chair leg, causing her to stumble.

Behind her Matt grasped her arm. "Watch out. You almost fell."

A nervous laugh tore from her chest. "Silly me."

Hurrying to the table, she dropped into her chair. Matt eased into the seat next to her and frowned. "What's the matter? Did something upset you?"

She darted a glance toward Toby and whispered in Matt's ear. "Did you see Toby?"

"I did. He didn't look too happy."

"He looked at me like he hated me." She clenched her fists in her lap. "He's coming this way."

Toby weaved between the tables toward Rachel and Matt. When he stopped at their table, he sat down into the chair next to her and turned in the seat. The smell of alcohol overwhelmed her.

"What'd I ever do to you 'cept keep your office clean?" His palm slapped the tabletop as the slurred words rolled from his mouth.

Rachel cast a nervous glance at the people who were staring at them. "Toby, you're drunk. Why don't we talk about this at the office?"

"I wanna talk 'bout it now."

Matt stood and stepped behind Toby's chair. "If you don't leave, I'm going to have to call Mr. Belmont. You don't want your boss to see you in this shape, do you?"

Toby pointed a shaking finger at Rachel. "It's all her fault. Told the police I shot somebody. I ain't never shot nobody in my life." His shrill voice echoed in the room.

Matt grabbed him by the arm and pulled him into a standing position. "Rachel didn't tell the police anything like that. After you sober up, you can talk to Rachel and she'll explain it all to you."

He jerked his arm free of Matt and staggered backward. He grabbed at the table behind him but only succeeded in knocking several plates and cups off as he fell to the floor. The clatter of breaking dishes sliced through the now silent room. A hundred pair of eyes seemed to bore into Rachel.

Cal rushed through the crowd toward their table. He stared at Toby on the floor surrounded by broken dishes, then looked at Matt. "What's going on over here?"

Matt reached down and pulled Toby to his feet but didn't let go of his arm. "I think Toby's had a little too much to drink." Toby swayed back and forth as he stared into Cal's angry face.

The muscle in Cal's jaw twitched as he looked down again at the dishes on the floor. When he raised his head, red splotches mottled his face. Rachel had seen that reaction once before from Cal when he had gotten angry at a reporter and fired him. She held her breath to see what Cal would say. When he spoke, his voice sounded calm. "Toby, I think you need to go home and sober up. The party's over for you tonight."

Toby's face crumpled at the soft words until he glanced at Rachel. Then the anger and hate she'd seen earlier returned. He tried to take a step toward her but Matt held him back. Toby balled his fist and shook it in her direction.

"What kind of Christmas do you think my family's going to have with this hanging over our heads? You can't go around ruining people's lives like that."

Rachel's heart broke at the anguish she saw in Toby's face. "Toby, please. I never accused you of anything. I'm sure the police questioned a lot of people after the shooting."

Cal grabbed Toby by the other arm. "Come on. I'm putting you in a cab and sending you home."

Toby pulled away from Cal and whirled to face Rachel. "She's ruined my Christmas."

Matt propelled Toby toward the exit with Cal holding him on the other side. Rachel glanced around at the *Beacon* employees who gaped at her. How could she face all these people at work?

It seemed an eternity before Matt came back to the table. He sat down and draped an arm over the back of her chair. "We got him in a cab and your boss paid the fare. He kept mumbling about a trip to Iowa."

"What was he talking about?"

"I asked Cal and he said Toby visits his brother every

Christmas. They spend their time hunting. It seems that Toby is quite a marksman and has an extensive gun collection."

Rachel's eyes grew wide. "Oh, Matt, do you think he could be the vigilante?"

Matt shrugged. "I don't know. He said he was supposed to leave tomorrow. I'll keep a check and make sure he's left town. Maybe with him out of the way, we can have some peace on the streets for Christmas."

"With Christmas just a week away, it would be a great present for the city if we could catch this killer."

Matt nodded. "I know. Maybe we'll get a break in the case."

From the front of the room Cal's voice rang out. "The staff tells me that the buffet line is open. Please help yourselves."

Rachel and Matt rose and joined those headed for the food. As they waited in line, Rachel couldn't tear her thoughts away from Toby. She'd always thought him such a kind man. Tonight he hadn't been the man she'd known since coming to the newspaper. His actions could have been those of an innocent man despondent over being wrongly accused. On the other hand, it could have been a carefully planned performance in an effort to gain sympathy and avoid suspicion.

Until she knew for sure which it was, she would keep a close watch on Toby.

The melody of "Silent Night" coming from the car's radio set the perfect mood for the drive home from the party. Matt glanced at Rachel, who was sitting with her eyes closed in the seat next to him, and thought how beautiful she'd been tonight. He'd never been as happy in his life as he was when he escorted her into that ballroom. That is, until Toby's accusations changed his mood. Then his policeman persona had taken over and he wanted to get the man as far away from Rachel as possible.

Even though the incident had put a damper on the beginning

of the evening, it had been perfect after that. He hadn't been able to take his eyes off Rachel the entire time. He wished the night didn't have to end.

He hummed along with the music from the radio and sensed her movement as she straightened. A smile curled his lips. "Did you go to sleep?"

She put her hand to her mouth to suppress a yawn and shook her head. "No, I was just thinking about how wonderful the party was." She snuggled into the leather seat and sighed. "Although I have to admit, these seats are so comfortable it makes me want to take a nap."

He cut his eyes toward her. "If you drift off, I'll wake you when we get to your apartment."

"Don't worry. I'm just enjoying this luxury. I got my car back today, and what I drive is a far cry from yours. I've never been in any vehicle that can come up to this. Your mother has great taste."

Matt tensed and gripped the steering wheel tighter. "Thanks. I'll tell her that if I ever hear from her. To me, it's just a car to get me somewhere."

Rachel reached her hand toward the dash and stroked it. "Well, let me know if you get tired of it and want to give it away. I'd be glad to take it off your hands."

Her voice held a teasing tone but he couldn't be sure if she was serious or not. He turned into the parking lot of her apartment building and stopped at the front door. He turned off the motor and swiveled to face her.

"My mother's good at giving presents. She just doesn't have time to follow up afterward."

Rachel smiled. "Well, I wish I could give presents like this. I would make Christmas a time to remember for my mother and sister."

Matt's mood was growing darker by the moment. Rachel had no idea of the warning signals going off in his brain. He needed to change the subject.

"Have you finished Christmas shopping for your family?"

She thought for a moment. "Almost. Cara has her heart set on a bracelet she saw one day when she went with Mama to the mall. She's really expecting to open it on Christmas morning."

Matt exhaled. So what he'd been praying for had finally happened. He'd wanted to know if Rachel was interested in him or his money. It shouldn't have come as a surprise to him that she was like all the other women he'd dated, only interested in his money, but it did. It always started out the same way—pretend to be interested in him, then suddenly there would be some item they needed but didn't have the money to buy.

He faced her. "So, do you want me to buy it for you?"

The smile on her face vanished and was replaced by a frown. "What?"

"The bracelet. You're asking me to buy it?"

Her forehead furrowed in tiny creases. "Matt, I don't understand."

He waved his hand in dismissal. "It's a simple question, Rachel. Evidently the bracelet is too expensive for you to buy and you're hinting for me to give you the money."

Her mouth gaped open and she shook her head slowly. "Matt, you're upsetting me. What are you talking about?"

"From the very beginning you've told me that you have to get a better job, you have to have more money. I tried to ignore the fact that money is so important to you because I wanted you to be different from the other women I've dated."

She licked her lips. "I've been honest with you about my feelings for Cara. When my mother's gone, I'll be all Cara has. So, yes, I need money to take care of her."

Now they were getting to the truth. "Well, I have money, Rachel. Lots of it."

"Th-that's n-nice for you, but I don't see what it has to do with me."

He ignored the tremor in her voice and leaned closer. "What do you see when you look at me, Rachel? A man you could love or someone who could give you cars and houses and an elegant lifestyle for you and your sister?" He hesitated. "And maybe, for starters, a bracelet?"

Her eyes grew wide. Then her face melted into a mask of anger that caused him to draw back. "Now I understand. You're accusing me of being a gold digger? For your information, I've already bought Cara the bracelet. I put it on layaway and paid it off. As for your money, I never gave it a thought one way or the other because it had nothing to do with me." She let her gaze travel over his face. "But now that I think about it, maybe I've been wrong to think money can solve my problems about taking care of Cara. It sure hasn't made you happy."

He frowned. "What are you talking about? I'm happy."

She shook her head. "I never realized how miserable you are, Matt. You blame your mother for giving you gifts that you obviously love, by the way. Did you ever stop to think that her gifts may be her way of showing you how much she does care? I never even received a card on my birthday from my father. And you gripe about what she gives you. Maybe she's not the only one at fault."

His heart dropped to the pit of his stomach. Had he been wrong about Rachel? "Rachel, let me—"

She held up her hand. "You've said enough, Matt. I'm sorry you have such a low opinion of me." Her lips trembled, and he could see tears in the corners of her eyes. "I respected you, but I'll have to tell my mother that she was wrong about you."

He swallowed. "What did she say?"

"She said that God would send me a man who could see below the surface and know what was really important in life. I thought you might be that man because you profess to be a Christian. But Christians shouldn't judge others when they have no idea what another person's life has been like. If you're an example of a Christian, maybe I'm better off without God."

He reeled from her words as she opened the car door. She was getting out and he had to stop her. Jumping from the car, he caught up with her before she entered the apartment building. He reached for her arm and turned her toward him.

"Rachel, please forgive me. I was wrong to say those things."

The tears rolled down her face and his heart broke. "Yes, you were wrong. But I was wrong to think I saw something in you that wasn't there."

"Rachel, we can work this out and get beyond it."

She shook her head. "No, we can't. I don't want to ever see you again. Don't call me. Don't try to get in touch with me. If you see me at a crime scene, don't try to talk to me. Just leave me alone."

She pulled away from him and ran into the building. He stood there for a moment before he trudged back to the car. When he climbed inside, he pounded his fists on the steering wheel. How could he have been so wrong? David had told him to let his heart guide him but he'd ended up trying to reason it out instead.

In the process he'd lost the one person who meant more to him than any other. He bowed his head in his hands. "God, help me make amends to Rachel. Show me what to do."

The words she'd spoken flashed in his mind. *If you're an example of a Christian, maybe I'm better off without God.*

He groaned as he realized how he had failed God. He knew Rachel's faith was weak and he should have given her a strong example of one who follows Christ. The fact that he might be the reason Rachel would never come back to God hurt him more than losing her.

He had to find a way to mend the horrible damage he'd done tonight.

SEVENTEEN

Ever since Friday night Matt had tried to reach Rachel, but she hadn't taken any of his calls. Now it was Monday morning and she still wouldn't answer. He leaned against the kitchen counter, his cell phone pressed to his ear, and listened to the rings on the other end. Her voice mail picked up and he repeated the message he'd left over and over.

"Rachel, this is Matt. I'm sorry about the things I said Friday night. Please give me a chance to apologize and make this up to you."

He ended the call, poured himself another cup of coffee and slumped into a chair in the breakfast nook of his spacious kitchen. One of the things he liked about his home best was the view of the lake from this room. Seeing God's handiwork in nature each morning seemed to give the day an extra boost.

There was no joy this morning as he studied the snow-covered ground leading to the dock at the back of his condo. The wind whipped the water into waves that rippled against the shore. A lone red bird perched on the edge of the dock and looked around as if wondering why he was alone on this cold morning.

Matt knew how the bird felt. Ever since Friday night, he'd felt like he had lost something he'd wanted for years. God had given him what he wanted, and he had messed up big time.

As he had done all weekend, he bowed his head and prayed for God to forgive him for harming Rachel's faith. Then he prayed for Rachel's forgiveness.

When he finished, he raised his head and checked the time. He had to be in court in an hour to testify in a case. If this day was anything like his usual court appearances, there would be lots of time to sit and wait. And downtime meant there would be lots of time to think about Rachel. He didn't know if he would make it through the day.

Rachel pulled the hood of her coat closer to her face and adjusted the sunglasses she wore as she entered the *Beacon*'s lobby. It was better to let her fellow employees wonder why she wore dark glasses on a snowy December day than to endure the stares her red eyes would invite.

On the elevator she ducked her head and leaned against the wall until the third floor stop. Once inside her office she hung up her coat, hurried to her desk and sank down in her chair. Pulling a compact from her purse, she slowly removed the glasses and studied her reflection in the mirror.

She snapped the compact closed and thrust it into her purse. The tears she'd shed over the weekend had left their mark on her face. She needed to put her argument with Matt out of her head. He was out of her life now and there was nothing she could do about it.

Her heart ached and tears threatened again. She wiped at her eyes and booted up her computer. Work, that's what she needed—something to take her mind off the words that had been spoken on Friday night.

Her cell's ringtone chimed and she pulled the phone from her purse. The caller ID flashed Matt's number and she laid the phone on her desk. He'd called all weekend but she hadn't answered. In time he would get the message and his calls would end.

The ringing stopped and she turned her attention back to

the computer. Within minutes, the phone rang again and she glanced at the displayed number. She sighed with relief and answered.

"Hi, Mama. How're you this morning?"

"I'm fine, but I was worried about you. I didn't hear from you all weekend. You didn't return any of my calls."

"I'm sorry. I was busy. I spent a lot of time at the Center on Saturday and Sunday. There's a young man there I'm trying to help."

Guilt pricked Rachel's conscience because she hadn't discussed Little Eddie with her mother. It would only upset her more. Her mother still hadn't recovered from the break-in at the apartment.

"Then I suppose you saw David."

"I did. He sends his love to you and Cara."

"And how about Matt? Was he at the Center with you?"

Rachel bit her lip. "No, Mama."

"Well, bring him back to see us soon."

Rachel knew if she didn't get off the phone, she would start crying again, and she wasn't ready to talk about her breakup with Matt.

"Uh, Mama, I have to go. I'll call you later. Okay?"

"Sure, darling. I love you."

"I love you, too, Mama."

Rachel flipped the phone closed. Before she could put it away, it rang again. Matt's number flashed. Should she answer or not? She wanted to hear his voice but she knew nothing could come of it.

She pushed the power button and watched the lit surface grow dark before she shoved the phone into her purse.

Nine hours later her workday had officially ended, but Rachel hadn't left. She'd stayed in her office most of the day writing a story that would run in tomorrow's paper.

Now reading what she'd written one last time, a sense of

pride overtook her. Her time with Little Eddie over the week-end had paid off. Her story about a young man wanting to put the gang life behind him and start life anew had a poignant ring to it. She hoped the desire she'd seen in Little Eddie for a clean slate and a new beginning would be evident to her readers.

After sending the story on its way to the copy editor, she rose and pulled her purse from the desk. The thought struck her that she had promised her mother earlier she'd call and she hadn't. She pulled the phone from her purse and turned it on when she realized it had been off all day. From the number of messages showing up, she'd received a lot of calls during that time. With a sigh she shoved the phone back in her purse and shook her head. She'd deal with that later.

She grabbed her coat and headed down the hallway to the elevator. The doors slid open. She was about to step in when the ringtone alerted her she had a call. Cal Belmont's number showed up on caller ID.

"Hi, Cal."

"Rachel." His voice held a hint of relief. "I just called your office but didn't get you. I hope you're not too far from the paper right now."

She stepped away from the elevator and switched the phone to her other ear. "No, I was in the hallway. Do you need something?"

"Yes. I'm out at Moon Lake Lodge for a meeting of the department heads with the newspaper owner. I left some papers on my desk that I really need. I would come back and get them, but we're getting ready to sit down for dinner before the meeting and I need to be here. Could you bring them to me?"

"Sure, Cal. Where are they?"

"There's a manila folder on my desk that's labeled December Meeting. Get it and bring it to me in the dining room at the lodge."

"I'll be there as soon as I can."

"Thank you, Rachel. I owe you for this."

Rachel chuckled. "Don't worry about it. I'm glad to help out. See you soon."

She retraced her steps down the hallway until she came to Cal's office. Stepping inside, she found the folder, scooped it up and headed back to the elevator.

As she waited for the doors to open, she almost wished she'd missed Cal's call. All she wanted was to go home and take a hot bath. Maybe her trip wouldn't take too long.

The drive out to Moon Lake Lodge wasn't something she enjoyed, especially in winter. Once you left the main highway, the winding, narrow road skirted the lake that in places nearly came up to the edge of the pavement. The newspaper had done a series of articles a year ago about the need for guardrails along the road, but the county hadn't seen fit to construct any as of yet.

When she reached her car, she tossed her purse and the folder on the seat next to her. Her phone rang and she looked at the caller ID. Matt was calling again. Ignoring the rings, she cranked the car on and headed toward Moon Lake Lodge.

He sat in his car and replayed Rachel's calls for the day. He almost laughed out loud as he listened to the pitiful tone of Matt Franklin's voice on Rachel's voice mail messages. He didn't know what happened between the two of them on Friday night, but from what he gathered, their budding romance had come to an end.

That only boded well for him. With Matt no longer at Rachel's side every time she left her office, she would be more vulnerable. All he had to do was bide his time for the perfect opportunity to get close enough for what he had planned.

Finally, he reached the end of Matt's pleadings and noticed that Rachel had received another phone call just minutes before. When Rachel identified the caller as her editor, he sat up straighter and listened with growing excitement.

With the call ended, he put the phone back in his pocket and smiled. This was what he'd been waiting for—Rachel in a deserted area without Matt Franklin to protect her. Anything could happen on a dark winter night in any of the dangerous places along Moon Lake Road. Especially to a nosy newspaper reporter who'd ruined his life.

He laughed and turned the ignition. "Don't worry, Rachel. You'll never know what hit you."

An hour and a half after leaving her office, Rachel exited Moon Lake Lodge. She stopped on the porch of the rustic hotel and pulled her coat tighter. The wind blowing off the lake sent its cold breath seeping into her pores and she shivered. Although the temperature always seemed much colder at the lake, she had never seen a more beautiful spot.

The snow-covered branches of the pine and spruce trees around the lodge and the full moon that hung over the lake reminded her of a line from a Carl Sandburg poem about a snowy woods and a dark evening. She smiled and basked in the picture-perfect scene that could very well be the cover of a Christmas card.

Stepping from the porch of the lodge, she ambled toward her car with thoughts of the approaching holiday. She could hardly wait to see the expression on Cara's face when she opened the bracelet on Christmas morning.

When she stopped at her car, she reached to open the door and glanced across the parking lot. Her hand froze on the handle. The peace of moments ago shattered at the sight of a car with a dented fender and chipped paint across the trunk parked nearby.

The drumbeat of her heart pounded in her ears as she jumped inside the car and locked the doors. She fumbled to turn the ignition and the motor roared to life. Backing out from the spot, she pulled the car into gear and sped toward the road. A glance in the rearview mirror sent chills down her spine. A car left the lodge and pulled into the road behind her.

Rachel took a deep breath. "Relax. Just because someone drove out behind me doesn't mean he's following my car."

Her thumping heart slowed its pace and her fingers loosened on the steering wheel. There was no need to panic. She'd keep an eye on the car behind her.

A mile later, the reflection of the lights still bobbed up and down in her mirror. Rachel chewed on her lip and tried to think. Maybe she could put some distance between them. She eased her foot down, increasing her speed. The vehicle behind her maintained the same space from her.

If she slowed, perhaps he would pass. Rachel let up on the accelerator. Whoever was driving that car had also slowed to keep the same space between them. For the next few miles she maintained a safe speed and kept an eye on the ever-present headlights.

She had just begun to relax when a sudden movement from behind caught her attention. Horrified, she watched the car ease to her rear and hover at her bumper. Without warning, a jolt from behind shot her car forward and she struggled to maintain control.

Ahead the road twisted and turned in the serpentine path it followed along the lake's edge. Rachel pressed her foot to the accelerator and surged into the first curve. She screamed as the car behind rammed her bumper again. Wrestling to keep the car on the road, she hunched over the steering wheel and pressed the gas pedal again. The car swerved around the next corner as if on two wheels.

In the mirror, the reflection of the headlights disappeared. Rachel waited for what would come next. The shape of a car materialized beside her, but she only glanced at it and back at the next curve in the road.

The screech of metal against metal vibrated in her head

as the car eased across the road's dividing line and struck the side of her car. She jerked the steering wheel to the left, hitting the vehicle, and felt it bounce away. With the short reprieve, she shot forward. She had to get away.

Within seconds, the driver recovered control and surged back to her side. This time it appeared he intended to finish what he'd started. She glanced down at the speedometer. At this high speed she would die if her car crashed into a tree.

Her tires crunched in the loose gravel at the side of the road, a signal she was losing this battle. With a final shove, the driver pushed her car from the road and onto the grassy area leading to the lake. Moonlight sparkled on the dark lake that beckoned Rachel to a watery grave.

She stomped the brake but it was too late. There was no way to stop. Rachel crossed her arms over her face, grabbed the shoulder belt with her right hand and screamed at the moment the car hit the water.

A cold liquid oozed over her feet. She lowered her arms and stared in horror at the water rising over her legs. She had to get out of the car before she drowned. But how?

Her mind raced. A year ago she'd covered a story on the drowning death of a drunken Lake City resident who had driven his car off a boat ramp. She searched her memory for what her research had revealed. As if she'd written the story yesterday, the information she'd studied returned.

The water around her feet deepened and she reached to unhook her seat belt. No, that was wrong. For the moment she had to remain anchored in one spot. The incoming water could move her away from the window. She had to focus on getting out of the car before it was too late.

If she was going to escape, she had to let the pressure between the inside and outside of the car stabilize. The only way to do that was to speed up the flow of water. With her seat belt still fastened, she felt for the door lock and pulled it up, then reached for the handle to roll down the window. For once she was glad to have an older car that didn't have power locks and windows.

She waited until the water was at chest level before she took several deep breaths and rolled down the window. Water surged into the car and pounded at her face. Within seconds the interior flooded, submerging her. She held her breath and willed herself to be patient until the car was completely flooded. The door wouldn't open until then.

After what seemed an eternity, she reached for the door handle and pushed the door open. Unbuckling her seat belt, she used the leverage to propel herself from the car.

Once outside the car she pushed off the side and swam upward. When she broke through the surface, she gulped air into her burning lungs. She could see the shore a short distance away and began to swim in that direction.

The water grew shallow and she realized she could stand. She rose to her feet and waded forward toward the beach. Her breath caught in her chest but she pushed her legs to move to safety.

She had almost reached shore when a figure on the beach came into view. "Are you okay?"

She tried to answer the man but her chattering teeth blocked her words.

He waded into the water and splashed toward her. She stopped. Something was wrong.

The man advanced. She gasped at the heavy jacket and the knit cap he wore—the clothing of the person who drove the car with the dented fender and chipped paint. Had she only escaped death by drowning to be murdered so close to safety?

A scream tore from her throat and she backed away. The lake's muddy bottom sucked at her feet and she fell backward. The water closed over her face again. She thought of Matt and the last words she'd said to him. How she wished she could take them back. For the first time in years, Rachel prayed.

EIGHTEEN

Strong hands clamped around Rachel's arms and pulled her up. Water trickled from her nose and she gasped for air. Even in the darkness she could make out the features of the person holding her by the arms. She stared into the face of the young man she'd seen in the lobby the day the Santa stole her purse.

He held her arm with one hand and put his other one around her shoulders. "Let's get you to shore. You're freezing."

Too tired to fight back, Rachel allowed herself to be led to the bank. Once on land she sank to her knees and panted for breath. The young man stooped beside her and spread his heavy jacket around her shoulders. "I was scared to death. I couldn't believe it when I saw that guy force you off the road."

His words drifted into her foggy brain and she frowned. "What?"

"The guy in the black SUV that forced you off the road. I couldn't believe it."

Rachel pulled the jacket tighter and shook her head. "Black SUV? You mean it wasn't you?"

His eyes widened. "Oh, you thought I was the one? No, it was somebody else."

Rachel put her hand on the side of her head. "But who?"

He shrugged. "I don't know. He pulled out when you left the lodge and I followed him."

New fear rushed through Rachel. "What were you doing following me?"

He glanced up at the road where his car idled. "Look, can't we talk about this in the car? You're freezing and I need to get you to a hospital. Then we need to call the police. I'll explain everything on the way."

Rachel hesitated. Should she go with this man who said someone else ran her off the road? She glanced at the highway but there wasn't another car in sight. It seemed she didn't have a choice. She needed to get where it was warm, and his car, even with the dented fender and chipped paint, looked inviting.

She pushed to her feet and tried to smile. "Then let's go, Mr.... I'm afraid I don't know your name."

"Hunter Ward. I'm a journalism student at the university."

He put his arm around Rachel and steadied her as they walked up the bank to his car. He pulled the door open but she stopped before she climbed inside. She turned to Hunter. "A journalism student?"

He nodded. "Yeah. There's a spot open on the school newspaper and I want it. I thought if I could work with you on those vigilante stories it might give me one up on another guy who's after the job. I've been trying to get my nerve up to ask you if I could hang out with you at work. Maybe act like an assistant so I can learn from you."

Rachel shivered in the cold again and got into the car. The heater blew against her feet, which felt like blocks of ice, and she pulled the jacket even tighter.

As Hunter drove toward the hospital, she studied his profile. "So you came to my office and my apartment and followed me to the lodge tonight just to ask for a job?"

He glanced at her. "It sounds stupid when you put it that way, but that's the truth."

Rachel shook her head in disbelief. "Did you ever stop to think that you could be accused of stalking? Why didn't you just make an appointment and come to see me?"

"I know I should have. That's why I went to your office. I was waiting for the elevator when you got off and stepped into the lobby. You looked so professional and almost unapproachable. I was afraid you'd laugh in my face."

Rachel turned in her seat to face him. "How did you find out where I live?"

"You can find anything on the internet." He glanced at her, then back at the road. "It was wrong of me to come to your apartment. I wasn't going to do anything but talk to you. When I saw you leaving with a man, I got out of there as fast as I could."

"And what about tonight?"

"I was waiting across the street from the newspaper office and I followed you out here. I was going to catch you when you came out, but you ran to your car so fast I didn't have a chance."

Rachel shook her head in exasperation. "You could have saved us both a lot of trouble if you'd just told me that first day what you wanted. I thought you were the vigilante."

The car swerved toward the road's shoulder with the sudden jerk of his hands. "What? You thought I was the vigilante?" He regained control of the car and sighed. "I sure messed things up, didn't I? Are you going to have me arrested for stalking?"

Rachel peered out the window at the stars twinkling in the sky. Peace flowed through her. A few minutes ago she'd thought she was dying. But she had lived. After being spared, she couldn't find it in her heart to condemn a young man who had dreams the same as hers of working on a big story.

She smiled at Hunter. "I may not like your method of doing

things but I understand you wanting to work on your paper. Besides, if you hadn't been there tonight, I might still be on the road waiting for a car and I could have frozen to death before one came along."

He straightened and smiled. "Then maybe you'll come to know I'm not such a bad guy after all."

"Maybe I will."

Rachel snuggled down in the seat and stuck her feet closer to the heater. Her tired body cried for sleep but she couldn't give in just yet. There were other things to be done.

When she'd thought she was dying, her thoughts had been on Matt and she'd prayed for the chance to tell him she was sorry for saying she didn't want to ever see him again. Right now that's all she did want. His calls today might mean that he felt the same way. Maybe God was going to give them the opportunity to mend what their angry words had torn apart.

Matt tossed the half-eaten piece of pizza back in the box on the coffee table and drained the last drop from the soda can. He reached for the television remote and muted the sound as a commercial filled the screen. For a week he'd looked forward to seeing the basketball game on TV tonight, but when he tuned in, he couldn't concentrate.

All he could think of was Rachel. He'd lost count of how many times he'd dialed her number today. Had she listened to any of his messages? She hadn't given any indication of it, because she hadn't returned his calls. If she didn't call by tomorrow, he was going to go to her office. She wouldn't be able to avoid him then.

He stood and reached for the pizza box just as his cell phone rang. Picking it up from the coffee table, he saw David Foreman's number displayed. Matt frowned. David never called him at home. He hoped there wasn't a problem at the Youth Center.

Matt flipped his phone open. "Hi, David. What's up?"

"Good evening, Matt."

There was something strange in the tone of David's voice. "Is something wrong?"

David cleared his throat. "I'm calling from the hospital to tell you Rachel has been in an accident."

Matt's heart thudded in his chest and he gripped the phone tighter. "What kind of accident?"

"She had taken some papers to her boss Cal out at Moon Lake Lodge. On the way back a car forced her off the road. Her car went into the lake. Thank goodness she was able to get out and swim to shore."

Matt rubbed his hand over his eyes. "Is—is she all right?"

"Physically she's going to be fine, but I'm not so sure about emotionally. She broke down when she saw her mother and me. She had trouble answering the police's questions. She's settled down some now."

Matt couldn't believe what he was hearing. He began to pace back and forth across the room. "Did the car get too close when he passed? Is that why she ran off the road?"

David took a deep breath. "No, Matt. Somebody tried to kill her. The police think it was the vigilante."

Matt stopped pacing and pounded his fist against the wall. "This is my fault. If we hadn't quarreled Friday night, I would have been with her."

"I didn't call so you could start blaming yourself. I called because Rachel asked me to."

Matt's mouth dropped open and he gulped. "She wanted me to know?"

"Yes. She wants to see you. We're in the emergency room. Can you come to the hospital?"

"I'm on my way. Thanks, David."

Flipping his phone closed, Matt grabbed his jacket off the chair where he'd thrown it when he got home and rushed to the door. As a policeman he was already planning how he would proceed with the investigation into finding the person who had tried to kill Rachel. But right now, he didn't want to be a policeman. He wanted to make sure that Rachel was all right and ask her to forgive him for the cruel words he'd spoken the last time he saw her.

Twenty minutes later, Matt rushed into the waiting room of the Lake City Hospital's emergency room. Rachel's mother, David and a young man Matt had never seen before rose from their chairs when they saw him.

Matt hurried toward them and wrapped his arms around Rachel's mother. "How is she?"

He could feel the tremors in her body as she hugged him. "She's going to be all right." She pulled back and blinked at the tears in her eyes. "Oh, Matt. I almost lost her tonight. I still can't believe it."

"What happened?"

Emily Long pointed to the young man standing beside her. "This is Hunter Ward. He's the one who brought Rachel to the hospital. I'll let him tell you."

Matt listened as Hunter repeated the events of the night. As Hunter told of his reasons for following Rachel, Matt clenched his fists and fought the urge to throttle the young college student. When Hunter finished, Matt took a deep breath.

"You made some mistakes, Hunter, but I'm glad you were there to get Rachel to safety." He glanced back at Emily. "Can I go see her now?"

Emily nodded. "You'll have to ask the receptionist at the desk if they'll let you into the emergency room area. They still have her back there, but the doctor came out and told us he thinks she'll be able to go home in a few hours."

Matt pulled out his badge and strode toward the receptionist. He flashed it in front of the woman. "I need to see Rachel Long."

The woman nodded and pointed to a set of swinging doors beside her desk. "Go through there and straight down the hall to the last room on the left. She's in there."

"Thanks."

Matt pushed through the doors and hurried inside the emergency room. A man in blue scrubs came toward him as if to stop him but Matt held up his badge and pushed around him. Nobody was going to stop him when he was this close to Rachel.

When he arrived at the last room on the left, the door stood open. Instead of rushing in, he hesitated. What if she really didn't want to see him?

Taking a deep breath, he stepped into the room and walked to the foot of her bed. Her eyes were closed and her blond hair lay spread out on her pillow. He'd never seen her face so pale. His heart dropped to the pit of his stomach. She'd barely escaped death tonight. She looked so vulnerable lying there, but he'd never thought her more beautiful.

He reached for a chair, pulled it next to her bed and sat down. Her hand rested on top of the blanket that covered her and he grasped it in both of his. "Rachel."

Her eyelids fluttered and she turned her head to stare at him. "Matt. I was afraid you wouldn't come."

Tears stung his eyes and he blinked. "Of course I came. Why wouldn't I?"

She frowned and swallowed. "I told you I didn't want to ever see you again but it wasn't true. Then you begged me to forgive you and I refused. I wouldn't even answer your calls."

He squeezed her hand tighter. "You had every right to put me in my place. What I said to you was unforgivable." He cleared his throat. "I know there's no excuse for how I acted. But I want to explain if you'll let me."

"All right."

For the next few minutes he told her how he'd grown up with only his staff around him, never his parents, and how every woman he'd ever dated had seen the money his family had as more important than a relationship with him. When he finished, she didn't say anything and he held his breath.

"In my heart I knew you weren't like that but I let my head take over. I'll do anything if you'll forgive me for the awful things I said."

She reached her free hand to rest it on top of his. "Tonight when my car went in the water, all I could think about was how I wanted to see you again. I prayed, Matt, for the first time in years. And God gave me some answers."

"What kind of answers?" Matt flinched not knowing what to expect.

She took a deep breath. "I thought you'd be like every other man I ever dated and end our relationship after you met Cara. When you didn't, I began to hope I'd found someone different. I love my sister and I'll do whatever I have to in the future to take care of her. But I don't think God wants me to put my life on hold. If He intends for me to provide for Cara, He'll take care of us. So I hope you'll forgive me and still be my friend."

A new sense of hope filled him. "I do forgive you. But I have to warn you. I want more from you than your friendship, Rachel. Do you think you can forgive me and let us see what the future might hold for us?"

She nodded. "I can."

He raised her hand to his mouth and kissed her fingers. "I'm so thankful you're all right. I'm not letting you out of my sight until this crazy killer is caught."

The door opened and Matt turned to see Rachel's mother entering the room. She smiled at the two of them and walked to the side of the bed. "The doctor says you can go home now. I brought a pair of jeans and a sweatshirt you left at my house when you spent the night. I'll help you get dressed so we can leave."

Matt rose but didn't let go of Rachel's hand. "Is she going to your house?"

Emily shook her head. "No, we'd talked about that before you arrived. A neighbor came over to stay with Cara and I'm going to stay with Rachel at her apartment." She put her hand on Rachel's head and stroked her hair. "I want to make sure that she's all right. Then we need to figure out the best way to protect her."

Matt nodded and smiled down at Rachel. "I'll be outside while you're getting ready to leave but I won't go far." He started for the door but turned back. "Emily, do you have your car here?"

"No, David picked me up."

"Then would you mind if I drove you and Rachel to her apartment? I want to be with her as long as I can."

Emily smiled. "Of course. David will understand. We'll be ready in a few minutes."

Matt walked into the hall, closed the door and slumped against the wall. He covered his face with his hands and said a prayer of thanks to God. After his argument with Rachel, he had thought she was lost to him. Tonight she'd almost been taken from him and her family for good. God had brought her through that terrifying experience and He had given them another chance to mend their broken relationship.

Now, Matt had to do everything in his power to see that a crazy killer didn't take it all away.

An hour later, Rachel glanced across her living room and studied her mother and Matt over the rim of her cocoa cup. The events of the night seemed to have taken as much of a toll on them as it had on her. She would never forget the fear on her mother's face when she'd come into her room at the hospital. And then Matt had arrived. Their conversation still echoed in Rachel's mind and sent ripples of happiness through her.

Matt set his cup on the coffee table. "So, I think you need to take a few days off and let us concentrate on catching this guy. Maybe Hunter can remember something about the car that followed you or we might find someone else who was in the parking lot when you left."

Her mother nodded. "I think that's a good idea. I can make arrangements for Cara and stay as long as I need."

Rachel shook her head. "I'm glad you're here tonight but you need to go home tomorrow. I have new locks on the door and Matt will come by every chance he can." She glanced at Matt. "You will do that, won't you?"

He smiled. "Just try and keep me away."

Her mother chuckled and set their cups on a tray. As she rose, she glanced out the sliding glass door that led to the balcony. "Oh, look, it's starting to snow again." She put the tray down, walked to the door and started to open it. "Let's get a better look."

Rachel sprang to her feet. "Don't go out on the balcony, Mama."

She turned in surprise. "Why?"

"Because it's not safe. The railing is loose. I've been after the superintendent to fix it and he keeps putting it off. I guess I was lucky to get him to change the locks."

Her mother backed away. "Thanks for telling me. I'll stay away from there while I'm here."

She disappeared into the kitchen. Rachel turned back to Matt. "You've been mighty quiet since we got home. Is something wrong?"

The muscle in his jaw twitched and he gritted his teeth. "I want to catch this guy more than I can tell you, Rachel. At first it was about the gang members he killed, but now it's like he blames you for telling your readers about him. I've got to stop him before something else happens."

"You'll get him, Matt. I know you will."

He raked his hand through his hair. "I just need a break." His cell phone rang and he pulled it from his pocket. "It's

Hunter Ward. We exchanged numbers at the hospital. I told him to call if he remembered anything."

"Maybe he did."

Matt flipped the phone open. "Hello." Matt listened for several minutes before he nodded. "Thanks, Hunter. Maybe this will help." Matt flipped the phone closed, pulled a notepad from his pocket and wrote something down.

"What did he say?'

"He thought he remembered the first two numbers of the SUV's license plate. They were 97 or 79 or maybe it was 90 or 99. He said it was hard to tell in the dark." Matt sighed. "That's not a lot of help. I wonder how many license plates fit those descriptions."

Rachel smiled and stifled a yawn. "If he's going to be a reporter, he better learn how to get his facts straight."

"You're right. I need to get out of here and let you get in bed." He took her hand and pulled her toward the door. Before he stepped outside, he turned and kissed her on the cheek. "Good night, Rachel. I'll see you tomorrow."

"Good. I can't wait." His gaze drifted over her face and she wanted to throw her arms around him. After a moment, she reached around him and opened the door. "Thank you for everything, Matt."

"Take care of yourself. I don't want to lose you."

Her breath caught in her throat and she could only smile as he disappeared out the door. She touched her cheek where his lips had kissed her and trembled at the memory. God had brought her through a terrible ordeal tonight, but He had blessed her with Matt's return. Now she had to make sure nothing happened to jeopardize their journey toward a new relationship.

NINETEEN

He walked into the kitchen and turned on the small television set on the counter. There was enough time to catch the local news before he had to leave. In fact, there was plenty of time to hear the sad report about the death of the *Lake City Beacon*'s favorite investigative reporter.

A commercial blared in the stillness of the morning and he sang along with the jingle advertising a car dealership. Maybe he would get a new car. With the side of his SUV banged up from sideswiping Rachel's car last night, he would have to do something. Right now it was covered with a tarp in the apartment's parking garage. It was a good thing he had the Jeep he used when he went camping. That would have to do until he decided about the SUV.

The TV station's logo introduced the opening of the news and he turned the volume up in anticipation of what he was sure would be their lead story. The morning news anchor picked up several pieces of paper lying on the desk in front of him and smiled into the camera.

"A local newspaper reporter escaped death last night when her car was forced off the road into Moon Lake."

The excitement he'd felt moments ago evaporated. He listened with growing anger to the miraculous escape, as the newscaster called it, of Rachel Long from her submerged car.

How could this have happened? He was sure she'd drowned, but she hadn't.

He picked up a cup he'd just pulled from the cabinet and hurled it across the room. Pacing back and forth in the small kitchen, he grew angrier by the second. He had to finish what he'd started, and he had to do it today.

There would be no more phone conversations for him to hear because her phone probably lay at the bottom of the lake. He'd learned in the last few days from what she and Matt had discussed that Little Eddie, the one person who could identify him, was at the Lake City Youth Center.

He walked into the living room and picked up the framed picture on the mantle. His brother's face smiled at him and he rubbed his fingers across the glass. "Don't worry. I'll make her pay. But first I have to visit Little Eddie."

Matt pushed his half-eaten lunch to the side of his desk and picked up the background check he'd run on Hunter Ward this morning. From what he'd found, Hunter's past didn't reveal any run-ins with the law, not even a speeding ticket. If he'd been looking at the report as a perspective employer, he would hire the young man without any reservations.

The fact remained, though, that he had a different reason for digging into the student's past. As a suspected stalker and possible murderer, Hunter bore more scrutiny. Matt had tried to impress that on him when he'd come in to sign a statement about the attempt on Rachel's life.

Hunter appeared remorseful now about following Rachel, and Matt wanted to be as objective as possible. But he found that hard. After all, Hunter had terrorized Rachel. Too bad Hunter hadn't thought about the consequences of his actions earlier.

His cell phone rang and he pulled it to his ear. "Hello."

"Hello, Matt."

His heart swelled at Rachel's soft voice. "Rachel, how are you feeling?"

"Much better. Mama let me sleep late this morning. I'm a little sore but glad to be here."

Matt pushed the thought from his head that Rachel had nearly died the night before. "Good. Just take it easy today. Don't worry about newspaper deadlines or vigilantes."

She laughed. "I won't."

He leaned back in his chair. "Your mother told me last night that she had to be home before lunch today because the lady keeping Cara was going out of town. Has she left yet?"

"Yes. David came about an hour ago to pick her up. She said you were going to drive me to her house after you got off work."

"I am, but you have to promise me you'll stay locked in that apartment until I get there."

She chuckled. "You don't have to worry about me. I'm not moving from here without you beside me."

Her words sent a warm rush through his body and he smiled. "I'll come as soon as I can get away."

"Good. Mama says you're to stay for dinner with us."

"I wouldn't miss it for the world. See you later."

Just as he disconnected the call, the office door opened and Philip walked in. He hung his coat on the rack by the door and rubbed his hands together. "It's getting colder out there but the snow's stopped."

Matt stood as Philip walked toward him. "How did it go out at the lodge? Were you able to find any witnesses who saw the car following Rachel from the parking lot?"

Philip shook his head. "I talked to everybody there. Of course some of them weren't on duty last night, but I was able to question some guests who were there. Nobody saw anything. I'm beginning to wonder if that Ward kid really ran Rachel off the road and made up the story about another car just to shift the suspicion off him. You questioned him this morning. What did you think?"

Matt's forehead wrinkled. "I guess it's possible, but I didn't see any new dents in his car. If he'd sideswiped Rachel, there should have been some damage."

Philip chuckled. "How could you tell? His car was so banged up, I couldn't tell the difference between what was new or old."

"I'm not through with him yet. I'll question him again."

The phone on Matt's desk rang, and he sighed as he glanced at the light flashing on line one. "Looks like dispatch has a case for us. I was hoping for a peaceful day." He picked up the receiver. "Hey, Mary Jo, what's up?'

"Matt, I've just sent two squad cars and an ambulance to the Lake City Youth Center. I think you and Philip need to go, too."

Shivers raced up Matt's spine. "What happened?"

"The director, David Foreman, just called. He had to drive a friend to her home and when he returned to the Center, he found a young man had been shot."

Philip inched closer. "What is it, Matt?"

Matt frowned and held up a restraining hand. "Who was shot?"

Matt heard some papers rattle before Mary Jo replied. "The victim is a young male named Eddie Haines." In the background Matt heard the dispatch radio crackle, then Mary Jo's response. "Sorry, Matt. That was one of the EMTs. The victim is still alive and they're taking him to the Lake City Hospital."

"We're on our way." Matt slammed down the phone and ran to get his coat. "Let's go, Philip. Somebody shot Little Eddie. They're taking him to the hospital."

Philip turned away and pulled his coat from the rack. "There's no need for both of us to go to the hospital. You go on and see if you find out anything there and I'll go to the shooting scene. Maybe I can get a lead on who shot him."

Matt nodded. "That's a good idea. I'll call you if he's able to talk any, but he may be dead before I get to the hospital."

As Matt ran down the hallway, he prayed that Little Eddie would live. He'd been so close to escaping his gang life, but someone hadn't wanted that to happen. Had the gang members found out where he was hiding and decided Little Eddie was a danger to them? Or had the vigilante found him? He and Philip had to find the answers to those questions.

Rachel switched off the television and tossed the remote on the coffee table. After surfing through the entire afternoon lineup, she'd found nothing interesting in the soap operas and talk shows. She rose from the couch and stretched her arms over her head. She could hardly wait until Matt got there to take her to her mother's house. Maybe a cup of coffee would make her feel better while she waited.

She sauntered into the kitchen and was about to pour herself a cup when the doorbell rang. Every muscle in her body tensed as she waited to see if it chimed again. She jumped when a fist pounded on the outside of the door.

Easing into the living room, she tiptoed to the door. "Who is it?"

"It's Philip Nolan."

Rachel leaned closer to the door and stared through the peephole at Philip standing in the hallway. She turned the lock and opened the door. "Philip, what are you doing here?"

"I'm afraid I've got some bad news."

Fear gripped her heart at the sad expression on his face. Had something happened to Matt? She reached out and drew Philip into the apartment. "What is it? Is it Matt?"

He shook his head. "No, it's not Matt. It's your source."

Her eyes grew wide. "Little Eddie?"

"Yes. Someone went into the Youth Center and shot him."

Rachel covered her face with her hands. "I-is he dead?"

"I think so. He's been taken to the hospital. Matt's there now. I was on my way to the Youth Center. But I thought you should know, so I came by to tell you."

Tears rolled from her eyes. "I can't believe this. I thought we were so careful. Do you know who did it?"

Philip shook his head. "No. It could have been a gang member because he was leaving or it could have been the vigilante."

She reached out and grasped Philip's arm. "I need to go to the hospital."

He patted her hand and smiled. "I don't think that's such a good idea. Matt's busy and I need to get to the crime scene. You should stay here until we know something for sure." He glanced past her toward the kitchen. "I hate to leave you upset like this. Before I go, can I get you something? A cup of coffee maybe?"

"I was just about to pour a cup when you arrived. Do you have time for some?"

He glanced at his watch. "I suppose so. The crime scene guys are busy right now, and I'd probably be in the way."

"Good. Come on in the kitchen."

Philip followed her from the room and stopped inside the kitchen door. "You have a nice apartment. Do you enjoy living here?"

"I do." She pointed for him to sit at the table and pulled two cups and saucers from the cabinet. Behind her his chair scraped the floor as he pulled it out. She poured him a cup of coffee, set it before him and stepped back to the counter. "I haven't done as much with the apartment as I planned because I've been so busy, but I'm going to do some painting after Christmas."

Philip's cup clinked against the saucer. "I hope you're not going to change the colors in the bathroom. I like them."

She chuckled. "No, I'm…" Turning slowly, she stared at him. "How do you know what the colors are in my bathroom?"

He smiled. "I know a lot about you, Rachel." A slight frown flashed across his face. "Oh, I almost forgot. I brought you a Christmas present." He slipped his hand in his pocket and pulled something out. With a smile he held out his open palm. "I wanted you to have this."

Rachel glanced at his hand and pressed her fist against her mouth to stifle the scream that rumbled in her throat. He stood and walked around the table—her cross necklace dangling from his outstretched fingers.

Cold fear raced through Rachel's veins at the hatred flashing in Philip's eyes, and she stumbled backward. She'd tried for weeks to discover the identity of the vigilante. Now she knew, but it would do her no good if she was dead. She had to live so that she could tell Matt. He had to know that the partner he had trusted and worked with was, in reality, the sadistic vigilante that had terrorized Lake City.

TWENTY

Matt sat beside David in the waiting area of the Lake City Hospital emergency room. There weren't as many people sitting around as there had been the night before when Rachel had been here. But then, as a policeman he knew that hospital emergency rooms tended to be busier at night than in the day.

David glanced at him. "What did the receptionist say when you told her you were a policeman?"

"She said they were trying to stabilize Little Eddie and she would let me know when the doctor said I could come back. I just hope he lives so I can talk to him." The receptionist stood and motioned for Matt. He hurried to her desk. "What is it?"

"The doctor says you can come back for a minute."

Matt strode through the doors where he had entered last night and was met in the hall by a tall man in green scrubs. "I'm Dr. Hailey. We're about to take our shooting victim to surgery, but he's awake and insists on seeing you before he goes. We've only got a few minutes, so make it quick."

Matt nodded and hurried into the room Dr. Hailey indicated. Little Eddie lay on the bed surrounded by machines with tubes and wires attached to his body. The beep of a heart monitor filled the room. Matt stopped beside him, stared down at the young gang member who'd wanted a better life and said a quick prayer for Little Eddie's survival.

Little Eddie's eyelids fluttered open and he blinked at Matt. "Glad you're here."

Matt leaned closer to the bed. "Who did this to you?"

Little Eddie's Adam's apple bobbed as he struggled to speak. "Santa Claus."

Matt frowned at the memory of a purse-snatching Santa. "Somebody in a Santa Claus suit?"

Little Eddie nodded. "He said he was there to finish what he started at the pizza parlor."

"What does that mean?"

Little Eddie coughed and the doctor entered the room. "We need to get him to surgery."

"No." Little Eddie coughed again. "Got to tell this. I seen the vigilante the night he killed my friend at the pizza parlor. Chased me but I jumped in a Dumpster to hide."

Matt glanced at the doctor. "Is there anything you can tell me that will help me find this Santa Claus?"

Little Eddie gulped a large breath. "I forgot 'bout his ring until I seen him pull the gun out. The shooter at the pizza parlor wore the same one."

"What kind of ring?"

A frown pulled at Little Eddie's forehead. "Funny lookin' one. It was gold and had a crown at the top with two hands under it. I never seen nothin' like it before."

Matt stood in stunned silence. A ring with a crown? Philip wore one that had passed to him when his brother died.

"Did he say anything else?"

"Yeah. Right before he pulled the trigger he said, 'This is payback for my brother.'"

The doctor stepped forward. "That's enough. We're going to surgery now."

Matt stepped out of the way as several nurses entered the room. He stumbled back down the hallway and through the swinging doors into the waiting room. He still couldn't believe what he'd just heard. Philip, the vigilante? There had to be an explanation. He rushed to the receptionist's desk.

"Is there a computer around here I can use? This is a police emergency."

The startled woman looked up and nodded. "There's one in the office in back of me. The girl who works in there is on break right now. You can use it."

Across the room David rose and came toward him. "Matt, what's wrong?"

"I'll tell you later, David. Right now I need to get on the internet."

Hurrying into the office behind the receptionist, Matt dropped into the chair at the computer and accessed the internet. He searched his mind for the name of the brother Philip had mentioned from time to time who died in Chicago. After a few seconds it popped into his mind—Michael Nolan.

Matt typed the name in the search engine and waited. Within minutes he'd accessed the obituary of Michael Nolan, a successful pediatrician who worked on his days off in a free clinic for destitute families in Chicago. The write-up listed Philip Nolan as the only family member.

Matt clicked back to the search page and found a newspaper article about the death. His eyes grew wide as he read the story detailing the murder of the prominent doctor who spent his spare time trying to make life better for the residents of inner-city areas. It said the police were still searching for the shooters who'd killed the doctor when he was caught in the cross fire between two rival street gangs.

"Philip's brother was killed by gang members?" Matt glanced around to see if anyone had heard his whispered words.

Had he been working alongside a killer for months and hadn't realized it? Matt jerked his cell phone from his pocket and dialed the head of the crime scene investigators who should be at the Center.

The chief investigator answered right away. "Hello."

"Jack, this is Matt Franklin. Is Philip there?"

"No, Matt. I haven't seen him. I was wondering where you guys were."

"Thanks, Jack. I'll get back to you."

Matt flipped his phone closed. Where could Philip be? He'd left the station to go to the Center. The truth hit him and he groaned. There could only be one place where he would be. Rachel's apartment.

He jumped to his feet and dialed her home phone. It rang until it went to her answering machine. He waited until the beep and then yelled into the phone, "Rachel, don't let Philip in. He's the vigilante. I'm on my way."

Matt disconnected the call and punched speed dial for dispatch. "I need backup at the Regency Apartments. Third floor." Without stopping, he ran through the waiting room past a startled David Foreman and to his car. He gunned the engine and careened from the parking lot. He had to get to Rachel before Philip did.

The phone on the kitchen counter rang and Rachel reached for it. Philip pulled a knife from his coat and waved it in her direction. "I wouldn't answer that if I were you."

She inched backward to put some space between the two of them and listened to Matt's voice warning her about Philip. When the message ended, Rachel stared at Philip. "What made you into a killer?"

His mouth hardened into a grim line. "My brother was killed in the cross fire of two gangs that were having a street war. When I saw how the Rangers and the Vipers were spreading out over our town, I decided I had to do something. My plan was to kill enough members to spark a war and let them kill each other off. It would've worked if it wasn't for you."

She curled her fingers to stop their trembling. "I don't understand."

"Only gang members were supposed to die. When that man on the sidewalk died at Pepper's Bar, I knew it was your fault. You'd turned me into a murderer just like they were. So I decided one more murder wouldn't matter."

"So you're the one who stole my purse, broke into my apartment and forced me into the lake last night?"

He chuckled and gave a little salute. "Guilty as charged, ma'am."

"B-but all those phone calls. How did you know so much about me?"

He laughed. "That was the most beautiful part of all. When I stole your purse, I downloaded spyware on your phone. I heard every conversation and read every text message. I knew your every move."

Anger boiled up in her. "You're a sick man, Philip, and I'm not going to let you get away with this."

His eyebrows arched and he glanced around the room. "And who's going to stop me? You? I don't think so." He lifted the knife and smiled. "This time I'm not using a gun. The noise might alert the neighbors."

He lunged for her, but Rachel ran around the opposite side of the table. Philip pushed a chair out of his way and advanced on her as she raced toward the front door. She twisted the lock and was about to open it when Philip's palm slammed against the door right above her head. His hand holding the knife plunged downward, sideswiping her arm. She twisted away from the door and stumbled backward.

He smiled and eased forward, the knife ready to strike. She held out her hands. "Philip, no."

"Come on, Rachel. You've wanted to meet the vigilante. Now you have. Too bad you won't be around to write a story about it."

Her foot struck the double doors leading to the balcony.

There was nowhere else to go but outside. Pushing the doors open, she stepped onto the snow-covered balcony. In the distance police sirens wailed. "Philip, the police are on their way. It'll be better for you if you give up now."

He laughed and followed her onto the balcony. "Don't be absurd, Rachel. They could be going anywhere."

Rachel cowered against the railing and felt it shake. With a gasp she straightened, but her throat refused to scream. She glanced at the ground three stories below and back to Philip. There was no escape.

"God, help me." The cry ripped from her throat.

A splintering crash echoed through the apartment and Philip whirled toward the sound.

Matt, his gun trained on Philip, burst through the open door and inched across the living room. "Philip, get away from her."

Philip glanced at Matt and back at Rachel. "You're not going to stop me, Matt. Not when I'm this close."

With the knife raised above his head, Philip lunged toward Rachel. A shot rang out and Philip clutched his chest. The knife clattered to the balcony floor. Stumbling forward, he fell against the balcony railing. His eyes grew wide with fear as the railing ripped loose from its supports. He grabbed for Rachel but she jerked free as he tumbled from the balcony toward the ground.

Rachel flailed her arms for something to steady her but there was nothing. Fighting to regain her balance, she teetered on the edge and stared at Philip's body hurtling downward. She screamed, "Matt!"

She swayed forward. Then two arms wrapped around her waist and pulled her to safety. Matt held her close and crooned in her ear. "Rachel, Rachel. You're safe now." He guided her back into the living room to the couch. "Sit here. I need to check on Philip."

She nodded, unable to speak, and sat there trembling as he

ran from the room. It seemed like hours before he reappeared. When he did, he sat down beside her and took her hand in his. "Philip's still alive. He's on his way to the hospital. He can't hurt you anymore."

Her fear returned at how close she'd come to death and tears gushed from her eyes. "Oh, Matt. If it wasn't for you, I'd be dead."

He put his arm around her and drew her against his chest. "I'll always be there for you, Rachel. I love you."

The words she'd wanted to hear for so long filled her with peace. She snuggled close to him and smiled. "I love you, too."

They loved each other. That's all she needed to know. There would be time later to sort out their problems. For now she just wanted to feel Matt next to her.

Four days later Rachel still could hardly believe how happy she was. She took a sip of her after-dinner coffee and snuggled into the cushions of her mother's living room couch. The events of earlier in the week hadn't spoiled this Christmas Day. It had been her happiest ever from the opening of presents to the huge dinner her mother prepared.

She thought of Little Eddie and hoped his mother had been able to spend time with him at the hospital this morning. His recovery and the family in another state who'd agreed to take him in had made this a happy Christmas for him, too.

Philip wasn't going to be quite so fortunate. In addition to the chest wound from the gunshot, Philip had also sustained severe injuries to his spine in the fall. He still had a long hospital stay and several surgeries ahead before he'd have to face the consequences of his crimes. She shivered at how close Philip had come to carrying out his plans and would have if not for Matt.

She glanced at Matt sitting beside her and smiled. He set his cup on the end table and rubbed his stomach. "I'm as stuffed as that turkey was an hour ago. Your mother is a great cook."

Rachel smiled. "I noticed you ate like a maniac. I imagine Christmas dinner at your house was a bigger occasion than ours."

He shook his head and frowned. "No, it wasn't, Rachel. This is the best Christmas I've ever had."

She scooted closer and grinned at him. "And just what makes this Christmas Day so special?"

He reached out and traced his finger down the side of her cheek. "Because I'm here with you. And because for the first time in my life, I'm in love. I never thought it would happen to me."

Tears blurred her vision. "I didn't think it would for me either."

He pulled his hand away and frowned. "And to think I almost messed it up. I'm sorry I accused you of those awful things."

She smiled. "It's all right, Matt. I think we've both laid our doubts to rest. After I escaped from my sinking car, I realized God had given me a chance at happiness and I'd almost let it slip away. I decided that I was going to put my life in His hands and let Him show me how to live without worrying about what might happen."

"I'm glad. I want that, too." He leaned back and stared at the Christmas tree and all the opened presents underneath. "I think Cara liked the bracelet you gave her."

Rachel laughed. "Not as much as she liked the perfume you gave her. Thank you for giving my mother and sister those gifts. You didn't have to do that."

"But I wanted to."

She reached up and touched the earrings he'd given her. "I love these earrings. Thank you."

He turned to face her. "I have one more present for you.

Well, I don't actually have it here but I have a promise of what's to come."

She sat up straighter. "You didn't have to get me anything else."

He pulled a small wrapped package from his pocket. "I hope you like it."

Rachel tore the package open to reveal a small plastic box. When she lifted the top, a folded piece of paper lay inside. She frowned. "What's this?"

He grinned. "Look at it."

Rachel reached inside and pulled out a page torn from a catalog. She gasped at the picture of the most beautiful diamond ring she'd ever seen. Stunned, she glanced up at Matt. "I don't understand."

He reached for her hand. "I didn't want to buy one until you could pick out the one you want. I love you, Rachel, and I want you to be my wife."

She stared in disbelief from the picture to Matt. "B-b-but, Matt. You know what my future may hold. Are you sure you can face the possibility that Cara may become my responsibility?"

He nodded. "You don't have to worry about Cara's future. As David once told me, what good is my money if I can't use it to help people?"

A tear trickled from her eye. "Are you sure?"

"I've never been surer of anything in my life. Not only do I love you, but I love your mother and sister, Rachel. Please marry me and let me be a part of this family."

The pleading look in his eyes sent a surge of happiness through her. "I love you, Matt. I want to marry you."

He pulled her toward him but let go just as Cara ran into the room. With a big smile on her face she squeezed between them on the couch and glanced from one to the other. "Merry Christmas!"

Matt and Rachel both draped an arm around Cara and hugged her.

Matt stared at Rachel over Cara's head. "It is a merry Christmas, Cara. The best one I've ever had."

* * * * *

Dear Reader,

Each December I get more excited as Christmas approaches. The decorations, shopping for gifts and the special foods make me feel like a child waiting for a visit from Santa Claus.

However, I've discovered there are people who are so troubled that they only want the hectic season to end. Many times it's because they've missed out on the joy that the reason for Christmas can bring.

In Isaiah 9:6, the prophet told of the birth of a baby who would bring hope and joy to mankind when he said, "For unto us a child is born, unto us a son is given: and the government shall be upon his shoulder: and his name shall be called Wonderful, Counseller, The mighty God, The Everlasting Father, The Prince of Peace."

It is my prayer that you have found His peace in your life.

Sandra Robbins

QUESTIONS FOR DISCUSSION

1. Since Rachel Long was a child, she has felt a great responsibility to her special-needs sister. Have you ever dealt with a family member or know someone who must have such care? How can all the needs within the family unit be met?

2. Matt Franklin grew up as a child of privilege, but he was unhappy. Have you ever thought money can solve all your problems? What does the Bible teach about money?

3. Rachel wanted a job that paid more money. Is there anything wrong with desiring to advance in your career?

4. Matt and Rachel were concerned over the problems their city faced because of the gangs who'd taken over some of the neighborhoods. Has your hometown experienced a rise in street gangs? How are the police handling the problem?

5. What can citizens do to keep gangs from infiltrating their neighborhoods?

6. What should parents and schools teach children about the effect gangs will have on their lives? What can be done to keep teenagers from being lured into gang life?

7. The villain's act of downloading spyware on Rachel's phone reminds us that we live in an age of advanced technology. How can parents protect their children from those who would prey on them in cyberspace?

REQUEST YOUR FREE BOOKS!

2 FREE RIVETING INSPIRATIONAL NOVELS
PLUS 2 FREE MYSTERY GIFTS

Love Inspired.
SUSPENSE

YES! Please send me 2 FREE Love Inspired® Suspense novels and my 2 FREE mystery gifts (gifts are worth about $10). After receiving them, if I don't wish to receive any more books, I can return the shipping statement marked "cancel." If I don't cancel, I will receive 4 brand-new novels every month and be billed just $4.24 per book in the U.S. or $4.74 per book in Canada. That's a saving of 20% off the cover price. It's quite a bargain! Shipping and handling is just 50¢ per book.* I understand that accepting the 2 free books and gifts places me under no obligation to buy anything. I can always return a shipment and cancel at any time. Even if I never buy another book, the two free books and gifts are mine to keep forever.

123/323 IDN E7QZ

Name	(PLEASE PRINT)	

Address		Apt. #

City	State/Prov.	Zip/Postal Code

Signature (if under 18, a parent or guardian must sign)

Mail to Steeple Hill Reader Service:
IN U.S.A.: P.O. Box 1867, Buffalo, NY 14240-1867
IN CANADA: P.O. Box 609, Fort Erie, Ontario L2A 5X3

Not valid for current subscribers to Love Inspired Suspense books.

Want to try two free books from another series?
Call 1-800-873-8635 or visit www.morefreebooks.com.

* Terms and prices subject to change without notice. Prices do not include applicable taxes. Sales tax applicable in N.Y. Canadian residents will be charged applicable provincial taxes and GST. Offer not valid in Quebec. This offer is limited to one order per household. All orders subject to approval. Credit or debit balances in a customer's account(s) may be offset by any other outstanding balance owed by or to the customer. Please allow 4 to 6 weeks for delivery. Offer available while quantities last.

Your Privacy: Steeple Hill Books is committed to protecting your privacy. Our Privacy Policy is available online at www.SteepleHill.com or upon request from the Reader Service. From time to time we make our lists of customers available to reputable third parties who may have a product or service of interest to you. If you would prefer we not share your name and address, please check here. ☐

Help us get it right—We strive for accurate, respectful and relevant communications. To clarify or modify your communication preferences, visit us at www.ReaderService.com/consumerschoice.

LISUS10R

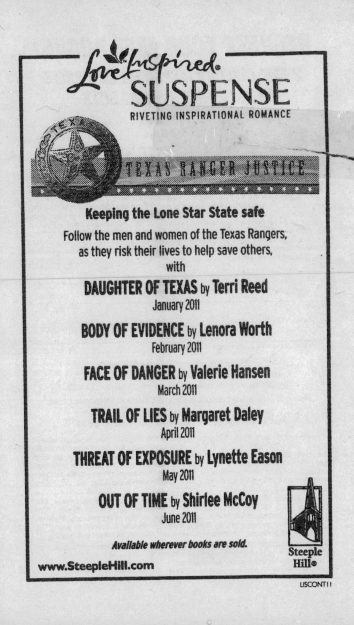

Love Inspired
SUSPENSE
RIVETING INSPIRATIONAL ROMANCE

TEXAS RANGER JUSTICE

Keeping the Lone Star State safe

Follow the men and women of the Texas Rangers,
as they risk their lives to help save others,
with

DAUGHTER OF TEXAS by **Terri Reed**
January 2011

BODY OF EVIDENCE by **Lenora Worth**
February 2011

FACE OF DANGER by **Valerie Hansen**
March 2011

TRAIL OF LIES by **Margaret Daley**
April 2011

THREAT OF EXPOSURE by **Lynette Eason**
May 2011

OUT OF TIME by **Shirlee McCoy**
June 2011

Available wherever books are sold.

www.SteepleHill.com

Steeple
Hill®

LISCONT11

Love Inspired SUSPENSE

TITLES AVAILABLE NEXT MONTH

Available January 11, 2011

8. Matt's judgment about Rachel's motives for a relationship with him was colored by his past experiences. Do you tend to judge people by what others have done to you or do you look below the surface of the individual to their true character?

9. When Matt and Rachel argued, he realized he was wrong and begged Rachel to forgive him. She refused. Have you ever ignored someone's plea for forgiveness? What does the Bible teach about forgiveness?

10. Matt longed to be part of a family that really cared about its members. Do you value your family? Do you get so wrapped up in your daily activities that you forget to tell them you love them?